Natural Bridge

A Journal of Contemporary Literature

Number 17 Spring 2007
University of Missouri–St. Louis

SENIOR & FOUNDING EDITOR
Steven Schreiner

GUEST EDITOR
John Dalton

EDITOR
Kenneth E. Harrison, Jr.

MANAGING EDITOR
Andrew Pryor

ASSISTANT EDITORS
Rewa Choueiri, Leontine Davidson, Mark Dischinger, George Fortier,
James Goodman, Susan LaBrier, Elizabeth Neale-Oestreicher,
Patti Smith-Jackson, Jeannine Vesser, Juliette Yancey

EDITORIAL BOARD
Jennifer MacKenzie, Steven Schreiner, Nanora Sweet,
Howard Schwartz, Mary Troy, Eamonn Wall

STAFF
Olivia Ayes, Capuchina Taylor

Cover Art: Sarah Giannobile, "Haunted" Printed with permission of the artist.

Composition and cover design by FOCUS/Graphics; page design by Adams Creative Services

Natural Bridge (ISSN 1525-9897) is published twice yearly by the Department of English, University of Missouri–St. Louis. The editors invite submissions of poetry, fiction, creative nonfiction, and translations during two periods each year: July 1–August 31 and November 1–December 31. Please address all correspondence to The Editors, *Natural Bridge*, Department of English, University of Missouri–St. Louis, One University Blvd., St. Louis, Missouri 63121. Include a self-addressed, stamped envelope. Visit us at www.umsl.edu/~natural. We do not accept electronic submissions.

Subscription rates in the United States for individuals are $15 for one year and $25 for two years; foreign rates for individuals are, respectively, $20 and $30. Subscription rates for institutions are $18 for one year and $30 for two years; foreign rates for institutions are, respectively, $22 and $38. Single issues are $8 (please include an additional $3 for single-copy international orders). See our insert for a subscription form.

Natural Bridge is distributed by Bernhard DeBoer, Inc., and is a member of the Council of Literary Magazines and Presses. It is indexed by *The Index of American Periodical Verse* and *The American Humanities Index*.

The publication of *Natural Bridge* is made possible by support from the Department of English of the University of Missouri–St. Louis and by a grant from the St. Louis Regional Arts Commission.

PRINT IN U.S.A. ON RECYCLED, ACID-FREE PAPER

Natural Bridge would like to thank the following donors, patrons, and friends for their very generous support:

Mr. Eric A. Bancks and Ms. Melissa Gurley Bancks
Ms. Denise P. Bogard
Ms. Gayla M. Chaney
Ms. Darcy Cummings
Ms. Carlotta M. Dalton
Mr. John H. Dalton and Ms. Jen Jen Chang
Ms. Amy S. Debrecht
Mr. and Mrs. Gene W. Doty
Mr. Mark M. and Ms. Deborah J. George
Rabbi James Goodman and Rabbi Susan Talve
Ms. Anne Hinds
Mr. and Mrs. Spencer E. Hurst
Mr. and Mrs. X. J. Kennedy
Mr. and Mrs. Timothy E. Leach
Mr. and Mrs. Brian M. Lindsey
Ms. Christine T. Portell
Ms. Nancy H. Powers
Ms. Liz Robbins
Mr. and Mrs. Kirk V. Swearingin
Dr. Nanora L. Sweet
Mrs. Delphine Troy
Ms. Mary D. Troy and Mr. Pierre Davis
Drs. Eamonn W. and Drucilla M. Wall
Ms. Barbara Yoder

CONTENTS

Poetry

Translations

Fiction

Essay

From The Guest Editor

It's fair to say that the world treats most established writers pretty well; think of the university readings and book signings and, for the more fortunate, award money and extended stays in artists' colonies, some of which offer the comforts and privacy of a first-class resort.

But for struggling or emerging writers it's another matter. Out in the "real world" their very presence is something of a puzzle. They may be a poet or fiction writer, but they have no books to prove it. They work jobs that don't sound particularly literary—file clerk, waiter, parking lot attendant. Perhaps they've been published in several or more literary magazines, but until they publish a book they exist in a gray area. They're working writers with no real status among readers or the literary community. The irony here—and it's often a knotty, bitter irony— is that emerging writers, as they work their multiple jobs and struggle to complete their first poetry or story collection or novel, are often among the most dedicated and worthy of any writers, established or not.

With this issue of *Natural Bridge* we've devoted a special section to six emerging writers who we think are richly deserving of your readership. Here's an opportunity to not only experience their work but to read their thoughts on the writing process. Yet even beyond these six chosen writers, we've selected what we believe to be a rich and compelling array of fiction, poetry, and non-fiction.

Natural Bridge is the literary journal of the University of Missouri—St. Louis MFA program. Each issue is compiled by a guest editor and a jury of wonderfully astute and committed graduate students from our writing program. They are listed as editorial assistants on the masthead of this issue, but they worked largely as equals and with great dedication and generosity. Here at *Natural Bridge* good works gets noticed. For all the struggling and emerging writers out there, this is a cause for hope.

—John Dalton

Linda Tomol Pennisi

American Legion, Independence Day

On the polished oak floor in two groups of four, the green-bereted girls move their bodies the way they've been taught. Two four-leafed clovers, they do their part for the boys who fight for their freedom in places with names that stick in the throat, and for those who fought in other wars, for some who sit on folding chairs to watch them bend and unfold their bodies in all directions. They do not know yet how their dancing matters.

Linda Tomol Pennisi

Ralph Edwards' Ballet Studio

This is not one of the five positions. Ballerinas do not lose control; they shape grief. What do you think the positions are for? If a blond ballerina plummets into the woods in her father's small plane, the others do not flail and saturate the room with sobs. They place the needle in its proper groove. They open blue cases and lace up their shoes. They swallow the light with their limbs. They bend the air into harps with their bodies.

Christopher Davis

In the Cold

1. *Indecent Docent*

"Kids, appreciate *moi*, slicking
up, in its mirror, this thinning

hair. The horny body,
in 'fine' paintings,

gets expressed abstractly,
a close-and-play, dusty:

your moma, boring.
Unlike *me*, dying.

Rub its hungry
flabby belly.

In Constable's cloud studies,
white mum blooms woo bees

no one sees. We
need to kiss, pee."

2. *Unmanly Mentor*

Fall. Balding, nodding to the full moon trapped out
past its prime, a stuck-up pearl in the cold blue beef

of God, I, snarling at a sausage distribution center,
whiffing doughnut, no, blossoming tea olive bush,

sex, sensitive deity,
turning against me,

slobbering,
yowling,

down boy,
chuckle,

"Raging neighbors, married fairies, cuckolds raking one another's
    faces, pages
of wives' dear diaries ripped loose, scattered like red leaves over mean
    streets,

swirl Peter Pan around on my rice cakes.
Take into a warm place. Huddle. Eat."

Christopher Davis

Opening

Tiberius Rex,
cringing, withdrew from Rome.
It victimized him.
Senators, grumbling,
could not forgive that goat's ungainly
terrified awkwardness, fear of long knives.

His will had been ripped.
Stepfather Caesar,
Augustus, god king,
planning the dynasty,
had ordered him, "Disown your own boy,
adopt my son-in-law, ignore, no, kill, wife."

Alone on Capri,
Tiberius, emperor
of all the cruel world,
paranoid, prayed in Greek
and stuffed his scream-numb mouth with drugs, dreams,
soothsayers easing his future stained red.

He was once brave, young.
Fighting in Parthia,
he'd seen colored flags
fluttering, miracles
of lightness, sun-struck silk: the Far East
opening, butterflies dancing for new gods.

He'd known to bow low.
Sadly, he laughed. What now?
Some curious Jew,
criminal, crucified,
preached, give back, gladly, blood, balls, brains, eyes
Caesar demands, but, dying, groaned why. Why?

Malcolm de Chazal

Corpus: From Head to Toe:
Selections from *Sens-Plastique*

Note: Malcolm de Chazal (1902–1981) was a Mauritian writer, painter, and visionary, known especially for his Sens-Plastique *(1948), a work consisting of several thousand aphorisms and pensées based on the idea that man and nature are entirely continuous and that all parts of the human body and all expressions of the human face, including their feelings, can actually be discerned in animals and plants. Chazal was hailed as a surrealist by André Breton, urged by Braque to express himself in images, and praised as an aphorist by W. H. Auden. Irving Weiss's two-volume translation of* Sens-Plastique *(Green Integer Books, 2007) is just out.*

Light is never dirty except in the human look.

No matter how common or physically unattractive a woman's other features, the certitude of her look turns her into a queen.

Illness splays out the voice.

The bosom is seated on the stool of the hips with the lower limbs for legs. The first chair came into the world as a symbol.

Emotion washes over the cheeks in waves, pulsates in the forehead, spouts in the lips, and curls round itself in the eyes.

Whenever the buttocks lose a certain amount of rotundity, they bear a vague resemblance to breasts. From a distance unusually full breasts look like buttocks. Drooping shoulders swing like hips. Very fat necks have calves. Puffy faces have bellies. Stout figures walk on thighs with their own cheeks. In wasted bodies the hands jerk like feet and the feet grope for the ground like hands. Touch a hamlike arm and it feels like a thigh. Some elbows are knees and knees sharp elbows. All those ankles for wrists and those delicate wrists instead of ankles. Sometimes toes dance like airy fingers, and then there are thumbs that press down with the firmness of toes. How many legs seem to come straight down out of shoulders, and how many people walk on air as if their legs were their arms. Nothing is only itself in the human body, as if the body were a house with all its parts screwed, nailed, and bolted in place. The human body is a magic dwelling in which the roof momentarily turns into the basement and the basement into the roof; where the open window is now a door ajar; where the ceiling sinks to the floor and the floor rises to the ceiling; where the right and left wings exchange places and the rooms exchange visits. The human body is a palace of symbols where all keys fit all doors, and we can rearrange all the partitions whenever we have a mind to. The human body is a puzzle of unlimited combinatorial possibilities.

A bird's visage is forever caught in its own profile because the beak is so much larger than the surrounding face. Seen straight-on any human face with an aquiline nose is a jumble of bird profiles.

Decapitated limbs are the most "alive"; the blow that strikes them exposes all their gestures at once. This is not the same as hiding your hands to show off your arms or hiding your arms to show off your hands.

The nose is the suspension point of the features. A voice stops abruptly, or is it an attack of reticence? The expression is held for a brief moment on the point of the nose like a dancer on her toes.

Grimacing takes over all the features except the eye, whose royal port refuses to admit it. An eye grimace is basically a rictus of the lids. The eye is the noblest part of the face, the soul's proscenium on the body's stage. Parapet and balcony overlooking invisibility. That part of the body nearest the divine presence. One can laugh at everything except immanence. The eye's majesty is total. Nobody laughs at the king on his throne—no matter how awful his physical defects or grotesque gestures, his majesty is overpowering. For the eye is essentially royal and majestic in itself. Crossed eyes do not evoke gales of laughter.

In order to appreciate the sensibility of the chin, look at the face upside down. Like an hourglass reversed, the sensibility of the lips that had a moment ago completely inundated the chin flows back into the lips, liberating the chin's hidden psychic force and reinvesting it with personality.

We no longer stick the little finger in our ears like our ancestors once did: too unsanitary. We don't use the index finger to point with: too impolite. We don't wear rings on our ring fingers: too unfashionable. Even the once powerful thumb has been displaced by more powerful devices. The human hand has lost its cleverness. The great middle finger is as ineffectual as the little finger. We might as well rename them all since their names no longer designate their functions. We might just as well number them like streets, and while we're at it simplify classifying the rest of our anatomy. Since the human body is the most perfect card catalog, why lose our way among all those useless entries.

The excitements of making love short-circuit our entire body. We feel as if our toes were in our head, we sense something of our own mouth in every other part of our body, our knee is in our shoulder, our shoulders are in our thighs, our arms have taken over our torso; and our loins have disappeared. Different parts of our body keep wandering all over like a rudderless boat. The trembling pleasures of making love displace our identification of our own sensations. We don't know where we are—we lose our sensory compass bearings, their relation to our true north, and fall into the confusion between nerves and senses of an infant being born. Sexual pleasure repeats all the sensations of birth in the body of an adult, the same ones we probably experience when we die, entering a new world in a new body, frenetically trying to orient ourselves, like someone lost in a thicket desperately searching for any sign of daylight. It may very well have been this corporeal disorder of members and parts, each continually becoming the other, that Adam experienced when he replaced the loss of one part of his body with a multiplicity of effigies of Eve from all the other parts. If not for our lasting memory of the Biblical origin of Eve from Adam's rib displacing his sense of bodily order, if it were not for its constant reinforcement by the voluptuousness of sex—sexual pleasure would never be anything but an individual experience in our bodies and five senses, never the experience of fusion within the self and with another that for an instant brings to us the Universal Enjoyment of all our senses as one sensation.

A pregnant woman breathes from her pelvis, while the creative spirit inside her "shoulder-breathes." The hips are upside down shoulders: look at a contortionist practically walking on his neck or think of how in the act of love—itself a double auto-creation—our thighs would "ride steeplechase" on our necks. Shoulders and hips are matched on the torso like the folded parts of a place card.

The tongue touches pliant food like the fourth finger of the hand. Anything sour it approaches like the little finger. Tongue turns into an index finger, directing food to the teeth whenever they are reluctant to begin chewing, and it thrusts food out of the mouth like a thumb. Tongue becomes a middle finger in order to curl around purées.

Elbows are our sidelong direction snobs: more right than right itself, more left than left—our *psychic* scouts on constant lookout. We elbow off the unwanted others who crowd us just as we walk shoulder to shoulder with our friends, calling them closer with the wireless intimacy of our upper bodies. The elbow is a physiological, psychological, and spiritual warning edge.

In plants the wrist is merely the hinge of the leaf. In animals the wrist is liquid, a ligament between the movement of arm and hand, not a joint in itself so much as a mutual extension of both. Only in humans does the wrist become instantaneously hard or soft at will according to whatever the gesture requires: solid or liquid, tense or relaxed in a flash, ready to square or circle in one single movement, flying or creeping on call, pawing or plodding, doing whatever a knee can do, as adroit as an ankle, connecting the neck's spherical movements with the shoulder joint's corkscrew gestures, uniting all finger actions in its microscopic flexions and equally enlarging the sheaf of articulations all the fingers are individually capable of. The wrist is master of every modulation of the pelvis, every slinking curve of the loins. It is the supreme crossroads of human gesture. The entire human body presides over and talks deaf-and-dumb language in the wrist's apparently soothing movements, for which finger and hand get all the credit and reward. The secret of the administrative acuity, the exact source of all this digital cleverness, the essential virtuosity we recognize in painter, sculptor, pianist, and gold-smith, the secret of the hand's entire ability, consists in one thing: making the wrist's power and adroitness flow into the articulation of the finger, making every finger joint a surrogate wrist, delegating some of the wrist's authority to the shoulders, so that every microscopic gesture in the smallest trick of the little finger becomes an exhibition of the entire body's force and character rather than a provincial gesture. In this way the brain doesn't need to go through "channels of command" and the soul can make immediate contact with life, freeing its spiritual-ity by means of the wrist, which would otherwise be an isthmus of rather elastic flesh across which troops of gesture pass with vacant faces and anesthetic bodies.

The hollow sounds of the eyes are our passport into the land of silence, where they speak the language of what we cannot say aloud. From the borderline of the eyes extends the vast gaze of the great silences. The silence in the eyes of babblers talks right into our ears. The mute look in babbling eyes is coiled around a soundless slender pin always ready to be tripped. The contraption will then disappear back into the look where its garrulousness always lies at the ready.

Surplus bodily movement is stored in the pelvis. An irregular gait swells it up. Floundering movements when you walk make you look like a creature in search of its hips, which can account for the pelvic waddle of trying to gather up all those gestures to return them to the universal depository of the hips.

—Translated from the French by Irving Weiss

Interview: Kevin Boyle

Kevin Boyle's book, *A Home for Wayward Girls*, won the New Issues Poetry contest and was published in 2005. His poems have appeared in *Alaska Quarterly, Colorado Review, Cottonwood, The Denver Quarterly, Michigan Quarterly Review, North American Review, Natural Bridge, Northwest Review, Poet Lore, Poetry East,* and *Virginia Quarterly Review. The Lullaby of History* won the Mary Belle Campbell Poetry Chapbook Prize and was published in 2002. He teaches at Elon University in North Carolina.

What sort of story or poem (in terms of subject matter, plot, theme) have you promised yourself you would never write?

I take everything my pen gives me.

Can you tell something about the origin of your poems, how they were written, where and what might have influenced them?

The poem about Abu Ghraib was influenced not by the pictures themselves, but by the thought that someday I might get numb to them; the poem about death came from my mother dying in the spring.

Who are some of your most formative teachers?

I think of the writers I read early on as being my most essential teachers: so Samuel Beckett, James Joyce, Walt Whitman, Pablo Neruda, Yeats, Seamus Heaney, C. K. Williams, Sylvia Plath, Robert Frost.

What must you do before you can sit down to write?

Get out of bed.

What's your cure for writer's block or getting stuck in a story?

The regular—allowing yourself to write poorly in order to oil the joints in the brain; once they're oiled, upping the ante.

What is the worst advice anyone has ever given you about writing that you followed before you realized it wasn't working?

Someone read a poem of mine that was pretty good, and I said I had written it after I had drunk a few beers. She said, "You should always do that." Bad advice.

What do you think of the idea that more people write poetry or literary fiction than read it?

Writing without reading is like cooking without eating.

What unique element or life experience do you bring to your writing that sets you apart from other writers?
I'm pretty normal: wife, kids, job, hair loss, etc. Perhaps what sets me apart is what Heaney calls his "first self"—as a boy I had a deep sense of rooted-ness in a large Irish-Catholic family in an immigrant-swollen neighborhood in Philadelphia.

When did you first begin to identify yourself as a writer?

Just this moment.

Kevin Boyle

THE RUB IN SPRING

Don't think the earth doesn't smile
as you walk upon it at night, doesn't look
up your dress as you spread the blanket
to lie down, doesn't want the ball
to roll deeper into the periwinkle and weeds.
The earth wants to open itself up
to you, and place you inside it, all
mouth, all saucy maw, common grounds,
and swallow you whole, whether wrapped
in clothes alone, or clothes and shroud,
clothes and polished wood, or naked
as a bone, and gnaw, slowly chew, take
its time with pulling you asunder, with
its mouth closed in such a mannerly way
no one hears a thing, no one finds
a crumb of you, no small souvenir or clue.

Kevin Boyle

Western Chant

Whenever I Abu Ghraib with you
against the grout in the shower, or take
the dog—part collie, part pinscher—for
a short Abu Ghraib to foul the avenue,
or even drink from the bowl made
in heat-resistant Abu Ghraib, I often think
of Abu Ghraib and how, from here
on out, whether I read a book of porn
published in Abu Ghraib or look
closely at fashion in *The Times*
with stoic models from the thin runways
of Abu Ghraib, things will be marked
by those photos from Abu Ghraib.
But with time, I'll relax, let my guard
down, and focus on the small Abu
Ghraib of the backyard, and the food
we prepare being charred at Abu Ghraib,
and the clothes we wear or strip off,
the teeth we chew with, filled with
the silver mined in Abu Ghraib,
and the miners themselves, little men
with a penchant for being down
the darkest shafts with canaries
from the provinces of Abu Ghraib,
everything, even after a year, becomes
laced with Abu Ghraib, something
the dark dogs sniff out at Abu Ghraib,
and my face, even when I see it
with my eyes closed, is stamped

Abu Ghraib, like a Made in USA tag,
and I lie back and see myself in
Abu Ghraib, first as the happy handler
yanking the chain, then as the black and white
man with the studded leash around his
neck, and I sense the small ray of
piercing light at the end of a long colonnade
is burning a hole, even if I do as I say
and don't move or blink, and it burns through
the skin and my shiny organs of bloat,
until it reaches the fortress-like Abu Ghraib
in the center of me. That's the point
at which I hear and begin to chant Abu Ghraib,
Abu Ghraib, to the Olympic music
of USA, USA, Abu Ghraib, USA.

Interview: Jack Garrett

Jack Garrett grew up in Los Angeles and now lives in Brooklyn. His work has appeared in *The Portland Review, Eureka, Dicey Brown, Bald Ego*, and *The New Orleans Review*. He also works as an audiobook narrator and occasional actor. "Topanga" is dedicated to Diana.

What sort of story or poem (in terms of subject matter, plot, theme) have you promised yourself you would never write?

A Millennial Messianic Serial Romance. But I've broken promises before.

What bit of advice do you wish someone had told you when you first began your vocation as a writer?

Drink lots of water, exercise, and marry a good-hearted woman with health insurance.

In my version of the world Flann O'Brien's *At Swim-Two-Birds* would be more widely read than the *Da Vinci Code*, John Cassavetes' *Faces* would win Best Picture at the Academy Awards and Petula Clark's "I Know a Place" would play at least once a day from every radio in the world.

Can you tell something about the origin of your piece, how it was written, where, what might have influenced it?

An article in the NY *Times* told of how the 9/11 death count had to be repeatedly revised downward because of false reports—including persons invented by those trying to cash in, as well as loved ones who just hadn't been heard from in a while; when I was a kid a flood washed through our house near the mouth of Topanga Creek; and I watched the towers fall from my bedroom window in Brooklyn.

Why do you think more good writing doesn't come out of prison where you would have so much time to write?

The seating is uncomfortable, the lighting dim, and the sex lousy.

How'd you get to be, you know, the way you are?

According to my mother, while still a free-floating soul I asked an angel to arrange for my (drunk, Irish) father to find and seduce my (naïve, distracted) mother. They got married, went to Mexico, and conceived me. Jesuits, Scientologists, and girlfriends took care of the rest.

Who are some of your most formative teachers?

Faulkner, Virginia Woolf, John Hawkes, Neil Young, and the nuns who taught me to read.

What must you do before you can sit down to write?

Remember that yesterday, or the day before, or some morning in my life, I wrote something I liked.

What do you think of the idea that more people write poetry or literary fiction than read it?

Jeez, can't we each read our own? That would at least make it even.

What is your most significant source of frustration as a writer?

My bad faith, laziness, and total lack of imagination.

What do you love most about the act of writing?

My bold brilliance.

What unique element or life experience do you bring to your writing that sets you apart from other writers?

I once appeared on Art Linkletter's "Kids Say the Darndest Things."

When did you first begin to identify yourself as a writer?

One day in kindergarten my friend Richie called me over to watch him kiss my girlfriend Linda behind the piano.

TOPANGA

She reported me missing. Didn't know where I was. Couldn't find me. Did she look? We were cousins. I'd pulled her pants down. Leaves were falling. Our mothers were sisters, mine dead. *Pressed* into me. Like into a book.—You ever been cold and hungry? she said. Sure, but then I went inside and ate.

What did she want with me? The canyon. We were little together. In the flood. Rescue pulleys, a basket of children, hanging over the waters, reeled to safety. Now, pushing 50, she showered at the beach. Her dusty family nudity. Waiting by the side of the road. They have buses out here now. A city bus goes up and down the Pacific Coast Highway. The MTA goes to Malibu. The MTA. On the PCH. Bleach blonde happy face, pressed into me.

—When I saw New York falling down, she said, I knew you must be in the middle of it. How else was I going to find you? Besides, it was a chance to get us some of that hero cash. What are you afraid of?

The Commission made me do it. Made me come. Mr. One, Ms. Two, Mrs. Three, the team. When One couldn't find me, Two rang; when Two gave up, Three came looking. Different faces, like people. Socio-psycho-politico interventionists. Whittling down the list. When the towers went down, names rolled over the threshold and piled on in sheaves: company rosters, payrolls, printouts. Steadily they fell away—6,310 to 4,562 to 3,206—chunks of duplicates, errors, frauds; of sad stories of cute little boys who had never existed; of real voices stammering, *I'm here, really, not under the rubble, not me, see? I was on the corner, on the train, in Jersey, hungover, overslept, I'm here, I'm really here, okay? Okay, I'm an asshole.*

Meanwhile, other names, new names, out of spacious skies in amber waves from the mountains to the prairies white with foam kept flying: one, two, three at a time, smacking the list—*ping, ping*—like red, white and blue paintballs: fakes mostly as the money poured in, but long lost friends and family too, the left behind hoping against hope to find a prodigal, even if ground to dust in a heap in Sodom. Like my cousin hoped. Because if not there, where? People had to be found. They'd picked a number. 3,000 slots to fill. Well, not quite. A little girl with a candle pronounced my name over the footprint last September before they found me. Number 2,769: hero to asshole.

My cousin lives on a legacy. When she turned 40, the shack on the cliff she grew up in sold for 100 times the price her father paid. 100 times. On a blanket of cash she slid down the canyon and lived like me. I'm on disability. I just can't concentrate. Or when I do, when I do the work and do it well, and do it quickly, and do it thoroughly, and clean up afterwards, expectations rise, my blood races, my face clenches, I snap. Fuck *you* and Fuck *you* and Fuck *you*. And I'm on the street by coffee break. I gave a doctor that look, he signed the papers, and I was left alone. The last free man on Madison Avenue.

Her mother, my aunt, got most of that 100 times. She lived in Italy. First thing out of my mouth,—*I* need to live in Italy.

—With my mom? said my cousin.

—Maybe.

—You'd slip in next to that?

—Why not, I said.

—She's got a flaccid ass now, cottage cheese.

—I eat that.

—Do you.

—I do, I like that, that flutter butter. Pocked and jiggly teardrop ass pacs. I'd come at that while she's turned around. If she's turned around I could forget she's my aunt long enough to make her face change so it's nothing like my aunt.

—You want me to call her? she said.

—Would you?

—No, she said. Not smiling now. Pressed into me. A leaf in a book.

Little Topanga Lane, still unpaved. The rocks, the ruts, the dust in the house. Dusting, dusting, make the sunbeams dance for Mom. A gutted schoolbus, a distempered dog, a wild-eyed pilgrim passes, raises the dust, disappears. Death, for a kid, daily, easy, like the dust. Turn a white sock brown. Where the house once stood my cousin camps. The hugging. Cousins are the strange of the family. So familiar—in manner, in memory, in faces our mothers—yet so off the map. Residents of string-theory Clevelands, Phoenixes, Bikini Atolls. Who *is* that? My knees, my nose, but her. Her and me, we're from here. And here we were again.

—All alone? I asked her.

—I had a dog.

—What kind?

—A brown one.

—A big one?

—Big as you, with a quick tongue. He kissed me on the mouth. I wanted to kiss him back, she said. I went to the clinic, I said Doctor, can I kiss my dog?

—You asked him that?

—That's what *he* said, she said. You're asking me this? he said. I said, Yes I am, speaking to you as my doctor I'm asking. He said there are people waiting. I said, Doctor, you're my doctor. He closed my chart and said, Yes you can kiss your dog. So I started kissing my dog.

—Nice, I said.

—But a month or so later I go back to the clinic. Doctor looks at me says, Here, what's this white bacterial growth, these eruptions and ulcerations in and around your mouth? You're asking me this? I said. *Thrush*, he said, his lips curling. You've got it, and I'll treat it, but I don't care to know more. So on my way out I told that waiting room, Kiss your dog, okay, but not *this* much.

The Commission bought my bus ticket. Urged me—One, Two and Three—See her, talk to her, reassure her, she's your Family. This is America. There is Freedom. Get your Closure. Go. They weren't angry with me, they weren't even angry with her. They were doing their job, making their own hero cash. Correcting the tally. I was off the list. I lived.—Now go live, they said. Nihilists.

She lived in sawhorse splendor. She had a wealth of desire beneath a roof of Visqueen. She said she liked living close to the Earth.

If she'd crawled in a hole she couldn't have indulged herself more.—You've got dust in your crack, I said.

—That's not dust, that's gray, she said, and pulled my head back down.

—Doesn't taste like it, I said. I fell asleep in her lap.

Her mother was a catalog model—May Co., Bullock's, Dicker & Dicker. But in the late '50s she'd done some art shots, front and rear; my cousin had found them and showed me. God, they were nice. No coy pose, no contemptuous challenge, no acting. Just an open face and some nicely groomed nude baby fat. 40 years ago my cousin gave me a magic marker, made me close my eyes and draw circles on those pictures, then made me kiss what was inside. My mouth got green. Look, I'd fuck her. Fly to Italy—how old could she be, 70? I'd fuck my aunt. What am I worried about, the neighbors? Weak stomach? Vaginal elasticity? God, strike me down if you want to, but I need to find my way.

In New York the girls get invitations, better offers, than a bad donut on the ferry. And the ones who don't don't touch my heart. Sounds perverse, but who said our hearts know what's good for us? Jiminy Cricket? Well, I've made my pilgrimages to the Magic Kingdom and crept down every nook and blind cranny in that paved-over orange grove and always found steel doors and chain-link. A little ice-plant, a little ivy maybe, but eventually razor wire. No passage to the interior, no penetrating the mystery, no fucking, in Disneyland.

Why remember? These brown hills we climbed. This lazy killing sun, phlegmy moon. Eucalyptus trees, long leaves, tall, rustle in the breeze, catch fire, and fall. My mother was beat. She lit the candles, muttered the Ferlinghetti and the Rexroth, wore the black catsuit with the snap-crotch. *Nepenthe!* she purred. My father was a salesman, World War II. They met out of uniform, on the beach. She put her rap on him and he could take a joke. But then it all went deep and gooey. Bang-bang wedding and a year in Canoga Park before she was back on the beach, little-dick me at her breast.

My World Trade Center. Get Born, Trade the Center of the World for a Name, Hop a Wall of Water and Ride. One day Jump. 20

years in New York and I'd hardly ever gone down there. Sometimes in winter. Pad around with a hand out to the few lumpy tourists in that cold stone saucer, spiral down to the dry fountain with the big brass ball—grand, ugly, future shock nostalgic—in my Mohican footwear. But there were restrooms underground, pretty clean. Hard to find a dry place to shit downtown. For the last free man on Wall Street.

—Why did you give them my name? I said.

—You could've been there, my cousin said. I didn't know you weren't. They kept upping the ante. I took a shot. The nation bled. Some gave all, all gave some. I gave you.

I was 10 when I'd pulled her pants down. She was 11. That was my first mistake. Taking her 11-year-old-ness. She would've offered me her 11-year-old-ness, in her good time. But she wouldn't be pulled down, not without a lifetime of tormented devotion. She screamed, she raged, as I took my little look, my little touch. What can a 10-year-old do with that touch? File it away for darker times. Darker and darker. 100 times 100 times.

Water fountains are vanishing, have you noticed? I gravely under-hydrate and still pee too much and still pee sitting. There are reason-ably dry stalls in Bryant Park, Penn Station, *Au Bon Pain* at 23rd and Lex *discrètement, et* certain branches of Barnes & Noble. In a pinch, the ferry. I was sitting on a bench in Battery Park near the terminal, when a 40-ish smiler came up to me. She was a hefty blonde in red sweatpants so I offered to give her directions.

She pointed at my face and said,—Did you know that in Christ's eye you are beloved?

—A mote or a beam? I said.

She simpered.—Matthew 7:3; I judge you not, lowly city Chris-tian.

—Be seated, I said and she smoothed her red bottom and tucked it into the slats. How would you like to take a ride on the ferry, I said. I'll buy you a bad donut. Her sweatpants were elastic, not drawstring, I noticed, easy to slip my fingers inside as I'd hold her in the fat boat, watching her eyes tear as we'd ply past Lady Liberty.—No one's got-ten into her since Nine-One-One, she'd drawl, and I'd pull her head down to my lap, a sanctioned means of comforting overstuffed witnesses for the Nazarene.

Instead, the boat left without us. Instead, she glanced down at her junction, rose up off the slats and said,—Be thee joyful, sinner, and another big beautiful ass wobbled out of my life.

Topanga. The MTA stops at the corner. Mobilizing The Assholes. Bent-flag mailboxes nailed in a row. When the creek rises the ink runs. Post cards. Love, Mom. Pressed into me.

—What did it feel like to be dead? she said. You could've walked around like the rose-up Jesus. You look like him.

—Mostly I get Manson.

—No, you're not the charmer.

I rolled away from her.—I don't like killers, I said. Carved in the sawhorse by my head was an image of the towers, my initials in one, hers in the other. She looked where I was looking.

—You could've been like that radical chick whose house blew up while she was taking a shower, she said. She dropped the soap, walked naked to a neighbor's, borrowed some clothes and went underground.

—Yeah, but I'm here, I said. On the face of the earth, in the sunshine and rain, with you.

Why I Left Los Angeles, by Richard Nixon. But that's not my question. Why didn't I come back? Because our little house in the canyon was gone? Because after the flood in '69 washed through it, and the winds in '73 burned it, and the mudslide in '77 buried it, and the quake in '80 swallowed it, and the punks in '82 scrawled with human feces the names of boy conquerors on what was left, I still saw her face in every scrap? You're asking me this? I carry a torch in a rainsquall for my home at the edge of the world. Now the MTA goes to Malibu I have no excuse.

She said,—You so fond of life?

I said,—You got a death wish?

She said,—I got *no* wish and need one. When's the last time *you* blew out the candles?

I sighed.—You can't know the last time you do something.

—Unless you say it is.

—What, this is my last cake, February 15, 1969?

—That's the one, she said. Remember what we wished?

—You waited too long.

—And all this time, she said, what have you been doing, if not waiting?

Autumn in Mannahatta. Leaves like burning pages fall. Sometimes I wonder why I came to this city of abrupt ends, except that my mother was young here. She wanted to end here. Abruptness, of stone to glass, of metal to metal, of walls to fists, of screams; or a change, a shift, a pigeon flapping out of the path of a truck; or the turn of a head, of a phrase, of anything too big, too quick, rips me open from end to end and I want to take and hit and slam and choke and throw from the roof. I want to tear things apart that turn suddenly.

—Remember when our Moms took us into the canyons? she said, looking to squeeze the heart out of me. Yes, I do. Sundays. Seminole Hot Springs, Paramount Ranch, Saddle Peak. Ceremonial rides. Hugging curves with no guardrails around the abyss. Our moms drank airplane gin and ate cold cuts and olives and spit the pits in arcs into the chasm. We parked on the shoulder and put down blankets and lay with our cheeks on our mothers' passed-out tenderness.

—Party's over, I said.

—Not quite, she said. Though we can't go where we used to.

—No, that's right, we can't, I said. And I can't fucking lie here all day in your homemade cave and talk to you about everything that ever happened to us and who we turned into because we can't do anything about it, we can't make it right, this is just how it is, this is it, this is the way we are.

—Okay, she said. But all I meant was, the road washed out, fell down the mountain. That place isn't there anymore.

—Oh.

—Which is all the better, she said. Because right here, at the end of the lane, at the bend in the creek, where they rescued us? The county built a culvert for storm run-off, and we can climb up that culvert with a king-size sheet, you and me, scramble up into the old arroyo, and we can take that big clean sheet and snap it out in the brush, and have our party there.

—Across the creek?

—I'll get beer, she said.

—In the arroyo.

—And lots of olives.

—Where the water comes down, I said.

—So?

—If it rains?

—The rattlesnakes will grab us and rattle us to higher ground. Listen, she said, of all the things we can't do, we can do this.

The morning sun in America shines last on its western edge and in February at 6 AM the sky is pitch dark in a little canyon by the sea. A boy and a girl, without an alarm or a word, will slip out of bed, and the boy will pee and the girl will plug in a space heater and they will shuffle into the kitchen and cut pieces of leftover birthday cake. They will get ready for school. But first they will sit and have breakfast.

On such a winter morning as they sit in the kitchen, something will have changed, but it takes the boy and girl some time to know it. This is the house the boy lives in but the girl often sleeps over and their morning routine is regular enough to be performed in a sleepy silence. It's only when they begin to speak this morning—actually, it's the girl who will say, *What's that?*—that they will know something is wrong. Because the boy will see the girl's head turn, her eyes meet his, her lips move, but he will hear nothing. And he'll say, *What?* but the girl won't hear him say it. And the boy will look at the girl, at her short lank hair over her pale brow and tired eyes now enormous, and a jolt of pure fear will shoot through him and his fingers and toes will tingle and he'll pee his pants a little though he's already peed.

For what has changed, what they've missed, is everything, everywhere, engulfing them, as constant and pervasive as the air they breathe, which is why they've missed it: the invasion and absolute dominion of a sound, an unbroken, annihilating roar. The boy and the girl look up and around and again at each other. Tears run down the girl's face but the boy's is dry. He gets up from the table, switches off the kitchen light, and opens the door.

In the dim light of the dawning gray day he looks out the back of the house to a place now gone, a place that has been less a backyard than a field of wild grasses bordered by a thick stand of tall bamboo and a wide patch of spearmint, a field stretching back to a line of gnarled chaparral which stood above the near bank of the creek that murmured down the canyon, a creek the boy and girl often played in, crossing in a few steps, hopping from rock to rock. But none of this, now, is there.

What the boy sees instead is a few ragged stalks of bamboo, leaning and bowing like beggars over a gleaming, crawling skin of mud. And where the mud ends, at the line where the chaparral had once been rooted high above the little creek, there is nothing—but water: a roiling, foaming, 30-foot wide, gray-green torrent plunging out of the arroyo, and thundering down the canyon.

The girl, just behind him, reaches around and puts the palm of her hand against the boy's chest. Her hand is cold, her mouth open, her face wet. She presses into him. The boy doesn't move, but watches the water. The near bank comes steadily closer as the flood rises and widens toward the house. Sharply, the girl claps the boy's chest and though she knows she can't be heard says to his neck, *Come*, and with trembling strength pulls him away from the door and leads him back to his mother's room and guides him to his mother's bed. In the muted light from around a pulled blind, the boy's mother lies on her side, buried in quilts, head wedged between yellowing pillows, her long straight hair spread above her as if she were already under water, her skin like glass around the deep blackness of her sleeping mask.

The girl presses, and the boy leans in, close enough to feel his mother's warm breath, and speaks into her ear.—*Mommy*, he says. His mother shifts, her chin lifts, she rolls onto her back. Her tongue appears briefly, the tip between her lips, licks a corner, then disappears.—*What, baby, what?* she says.

The boy, innocent still, stares at her changeless face. The girl presses again. He leans.—*Mommy, wake up*, his lips moist in her ear.

And though the water keeps coming, keeps creeping up the field of mud toward the window, and though the air itself announces its coming and the coming of an end, the boy, bending close to her face, hears only his mother when she says, smiling slightly beneath her mask,—*It's okay, baby. You can do it. You go ahead without me.*

And the boy stands straight. And he looks down at his mother and he would hug her and say goodbye, but he doesn't. The girl is there. His mother he could no longer have, but the girl he might, and he takes the girl's hand, cold in his, and he takes her out of the house.

Andy Cox

Childhood

It involved horses and a house we thought haunted but only an old woman lived there who could not speak English. It involved a favorite bicycle and certain tree-lined streets and lost chances and the rustle of the leaves on a hot dry day. It involved building a fort in the woods behind the cemetery and wind chimes tinkling on a distant porch. Other than that we're not sure anything else is worth mentioning. Other than that we're not sure what else to say. Other than that we are going to keep our mouths shut. Other than that we are going to let the cat from next door walk leisurely through the brown yard with the mouse tail dangling from its mouth.

Andy Cox

CHAIN OF EVENTS

He liked how she left her shoes on. Later they talked. Later she went home. Later they never saw each other again. Later each of their lives took an unexpected turn. This left each with a certain attitude towards daily events. Later they got old and did not recognize themselves in the mirror.

Andy Cox

Look

You and the horse gallop through the woods on the narrow trail and it does not matter, the risk and the spill that is about to happen but now there is only the velocity and the blurring trees and the sound hooves make. Pain, the pain comes to this: it's worth it, this you and the horse and the trail that leads you, this wild turkey about to scurry across and spook the horse; it is worth it, this ache. Pain, the pain comes to this: scream all you want to, cry because it is worth it, you and the horse galloping and not looking back.

Ron Savage

Hollywood Suicides

October 1961
Nevada

Most of the horses are sick and will die soon. That's what the veterinarian tells Johnny Boy, the director. It's what Johnny Boy tells the crew and his principals. They have practiced the scene five or six times. It begins with a small plane chasing the wild mustangs toward the actors. The actors ride in the flatbed of a truck and try to rope the animals; once or twice an actor actually does this, but some of the horses stumble and get dragged before the truck can stop. The real cowboy, the production company's hired advisor, says to the director, Yeah, you got it right, bud, exactly to a T. That's your dog food round up.

November 1940
Ravensbruck

There are 10,000 women here, scared, emaciated women. She has watched them cut and sew their blankets into Nazi uniforms. They march around the barrack with high kicking goose steps. Jews are telling other Jews what to do. Make your bed, they say. Scrub your floor, they say. The place smells of stale sweat and urine. She writes in her journal: These frightened women pretend they are the people who frighten them. They have become our guards. Her name is Irma Woetzel; she will be eighteen this January. She is sticks and skin. Her eyes are large and dark and give her a shocked look. Irma was a first-year medical student at the University of Freiburg. She adores Freud and Otto Rank, Eugen Bleuler and Carl Jung. She writes, Some of us try to stop our suffering in ways that are worse than the disease.

October 1961
Nevada

N. J. has barricaded herself inside her Airstream. A clear glass vase of orange, red, and white Peruvian orchids is on the small Formica table in the breakfast nook. The card reads, Oh, to be in Brentwood by the pool! We all love you, sweetheart. Johnny Boy. A warm desert breeze rushes through the open window of her trailer. It smells like Redondo Beach without the water. They've been waiting for her for over an hour now but N. J. refuses to leave her trailer and be humiliated. She has been drinking Dom Perignon '53, what she thinks movie stars ought to drink. She sometimes mixes this with Nembutal but not today. Or perhaps today, don't ask her to remember. N. J. is tinier than people expect, a barefoot 5' 4". She is also more beautiful than they expect. Men who meet her forget what language they speak; women, too. They see her as an orphan with platinum hair and hungry blue eyes. They see her as the girl next door who will never live next door to them. It's an unrelenting beauty, that opened mouth, Holy Shit sort of beauty.

Her soon to be ex-husband has written her a screenplay. Her Valentine's Day present, he says. And she hates it. And she hates him. And she hates this place. Jesus, she hates this hot, barren place. Who writes a play about catching horses and turning them into dog food? Who does that? She wishes her husband were dead. Maybe not dead. Maybe wounded.

December 1942
Ravensbruck

Irma sits cross-legged on a narrow upper bunk made of wooden slats. The beds are stacked three high against the wall. Her barrack is crowded and gray. That familiar odor of sweat and urine permeates everything. Irma has joined the resistance and teaches biology in their underground high school. She is preparing her lecture for this evening.

The prisoners are calling her Dr. Woetzel. I'm only a first-year student, Irma reminds them. You're all we've got, they tell her. Being a doctor here is never easy. Being called a doctor and not being one is worse. At night the SS goes from barrack to barrack and shoots the sick and weaker prisoners. Irma can hear the distant gunfire from her bunk. The SS guards are all women, a hundred and fifty of them. The wardress is Elfriede Muller, who is nicknamed, The Beast of Ravensbruck. Every time the SS shoots a sick prisoner, someone will say to Irma, Aren't you supposed to help sick people get better? How can you call yourself a doctor?

October 1961
Nevada

Johnny, the director, taps on the door of her Airstream. He says, Time and money, sweetheart. We all love you, okay? Precious? Hello? She adores Johnny Boy. He is a giant Irishman with long delicate fingers and nails that stay manicured. He has a voice that rumbles in her chest like a stereo. She isn't ready to talk to him, though. Her leading man is twenty-five years older than N. J. and he is in love with her. All the signs are there. He has become too amusing. His flattery has no end or shame. N. J. heard him order the crew to keep their anger and their opinions of her to themselves. He likes to bring her things, a soda, a silk scarf for the desert evenings, a small flowering cactus, a morning cup of coffee (three creams, two sugars). He smells better than he used to, not that he ever smelled bad. He also insists on doing his own stunts. A sixty-year-old man who has heart problems and smokes Chesterfields shouldn't do his own stunts. But what can you say? If he were twelve, he would ride his bike for her with no hands.

April 1958
New York City

Dr. Woetzel wakes, screaming. She has a window open in her bedroom which is seven floors above the street on Central Park West. Something backfired, a car, a bus, a truck, something. The backfire became one of the SS women shooting a sick prisoner. She can feel her heartbeat pumping against her chest. Old barrack critics come to the foreground and scold her. Aren't you supposed to help sick people get better? How can you call yourself a doctor? Irma Woetzel releases a little breath and looks around her moonlit bedroom. This isn't Ravens-bruck, no wooden bunks here, no smell of urine or stale sweat. The scent is pine potpourri. The sheets are Egyptian cotton.

Each year is a miracle, that's the way it seems; nothing Dr. Woet-zel could have imagined. They were liberated by the Allies on April 30, 1945. 130,000 women passed through Ravensbruck. Irma was one of 40,000 survivors. After finishing her medical studies at the University of Edinburgh, she wrote to Jacques Lacan and he accepted her for psy-choanalytic training at Hospital Sainte Anne in Paris. She impressed Lacan and, on his recommendation, The New York Psychoanalytic Institute offered to bring her to America. God was making up for a bad start.

One of the women at Ravensbruck married an American second lieutenant. He's an orthodontist from Los Angeles. The woman is always urging Irma to come and live in California. We've got palm trees and beautiful boys, she writes. We've got sunny skies and beaches. Dr. Woetzel doesn't know. She loves her New York patients. They are artsy types, painters, writers, theater people. All of them start by think-ing psychoanalysis will take their creativity along with their neurosis. They like pointing to successful crazy people. Van Gogh is a favorite. Dr. Woetzel's answer doesn't vary. A neurosis ties down the soul, she says. Then she grins and claps her palms together, saying: Think what Van Gogh might have done if he'd kept both his ears. In a recent phone call, her friend said California was heaven for analysts and not to worry. The friend said, Darling, you must trust me, you'll fit right in. We have movie stars.

October 1961
Nevada

The crew, director, and principles are staying at Reno's Mapes Hotel. N. J. and her annoying screenwriter soon to be ex-husband have a six-room suite on the top floor. I love their Art Deco, N. J. says and does a little twirl in the sitting area. Don't you just love it? I feel like I'm in one of those Fred Astaire/Ginger Roger movies. Her husband says, Art Deco is French. We have Early American Modernism. His arms are thin with dark hair. Serious black glasses mask a narrow face. He is on his way out and shuts the door behind him. The movie star isn't a dumb blonde. She knows he is having an affair with the publicity photographer. She hopes his dick falls off. Maybe not falls off. Maybe a rash.

Tomorrow her sixty-year-old leading man will be dragged across the desert floor by a wild horse. Her leading man smokes Chesterfields and has a bad heart. N. J. has pleaded with him about this. You don't need to do it, daddy, she says. That's what she calls him. Daddy. He doesn't much care for it. She says, You're the king, daddy. You don't have to prove anything to anybody. He does that bemused half-smile, that arched eyebrow, those crinkles in the corners of his eyes. She has seen his smile a hundred times, a thousand. Friday nights, Saturday matinees, his smile came after the Movietone News and the Tom and Jerry cartoon. His smile brought back dark theaters and greasy popcorn. I'm not your daddy, he told her. How could any man in his right mind be your daddy?

N. J. is curled up on a two-seater Biermeier sofa in her hotel suite. The sofa has pale blue silk upholstery and a polished teakwood frame. She wears a white terry cloth bathrobe. Her legs are tucked beneath her and a black telephone is next to her left hand. N. J. wants to call L.A. at 1:20 AM and get some advice. Her therapist would know what to do. Dr. Woetzel understands everything.

April 1960
Los Angeles

You've been to a lot of therapists, Dr. Woetzel says while glancing through her new patient's file. The California practice has grown beyond her best fantasy. She sees more stars than William Morris. Now the doctor notices a tremor in her own hand. She is aroused by this woman, this new patient. That has never happened, not in Ravensbruck or Scotland, not in Paris or New York. And it isn't just the patient's beauty. Dr. Woetzel is becoming used to that sort of beauty. No, it's something behind the eyes. The eyes pull at the doctor like a child craving an unreachable toy. Dr. Woetzel finishes the patient's file and says, You've tried to hurt yourself on five different occasions. Always pills and alcohol. And always about men. Dr. Woetzel says this as if thinking out loud, a problem for them to solve. The patient looks down at her hands. The fingernails are manicured and cherry red and posed on her crossed knee. Today she wears a short white skirt and matching jacket. She says, When you're in the movies, they don't like you cutting on yourself. Dr. Woetzel wants to know if she thinks about that. The patient rolls her eyes and fingers her platinum hair. God, no, the patient says. Then she says, People don't pay money to see a woman with scars. Dr. Woetzel grins and claps her palms together and tells her patient how that's the best answer she has heard today. Tears glisten along the rims of the patient's eyes. Look at me, she whispers and retrieves a tissue from her white leather purse.

October 1961
Nevada

The sixty-year-old leading man has just walked onto the set, the white Nevada sand, the unstoppable morning sun. He has on his leather chaps and vest, a dark long sleeve shirt and a bandana. A coiled rope is in his left hand. He nods to N. J. as he passes her, even winks. This man she likes to call "daddy" remarried in 1955, his fifth wife, and they're expecting a child in February. He's never been a cheater but N. J. has stirred him in an odd way. She reminds him of his third wife, the actress. That was life at its happiest. But he won't go to bed with N. J., not that he doesn't want to. He won't compete with the playwright, either, not that he can't. He just needs to let N. J. know he's not her daddy. It's movie number seventy-two for him. Some of the crew stop their work to applaud.

May 1962
Los Angeles

This afternoon Dr. Woetzel is listening to N. J. but realizes Ravensbruck has entered her mind. The doctor is remembering the muted gunfire; the nights the SS women marched from barrack to barrack, shooting the sick. She is remembering the frightened ones who had whispered to her, Aren't you supposed to help sick people get better? How can you call yourself a doctor?

Bright yellow sunlight from her office window crosses the polished oak floors and the red and white Persian rug. The smell of leather furniture and old books mix with the heavy scent of N. J.'s Chanel.

The man had a heart condition, N. J. is saying. She is wearing an Oleg Cassini black linen suit and ruby red pumps. Her fingernails and lips match her shoes. She says, He smoked Chesterfields. He had one of those awful phlegmy coughs, you know? When he laughed, he had it. You can't be sixty and have heart problems and expect to live through that. Can you? Am I right?

October 1961
Nevada

Everything has become background except him and the horse. That's the way it works. He is no Brando, the method and that Actor's Studio soul-searching crap doesn't interest him. What happens now is what always happens. He doesn't think about it; he doesn't analyze it. Things drop away. N. J., Johnny Boy, the crew, his pregnant wife, the cheese Danish and coffee he had for breakfast, things drop away. A loop of rope has fallen about the horse's black shiny neck. The horse's whinny is more like a scream. It rears up, front hooves stabbing at the hot desert air. That rebellion, that abrupt strength, surprises him. The animal's saliva patters his forehead and cheeks. Its hooves are above his head, raking, thrusting. He imagines the hooves cutting his face, breaking his nose or his cheekbone. It annoys him that he is having anxiety about his looks and career. He yanks down on the rope and believes he can see panic tremble the black mustang's right flank. The animal raises its front legs again but rears back too far and falls on its side. The horse squeals. White sand balloons like a storm. The leading man just stands there holding the lasso. He wonders if doing his own stunts was a good idea. Then the horse is up and running. The rope goes taut and the man's balance is lost and he tumbles onto the white sand. The morning sun begins to burn his shoulders and neck. Hot stinging sand pelts his face. He squints his eyes and watches the black mustang's galloping hind legs. From some other world he hears Johnny boy yelling, Hang on! Hang on as long as you can, kiddo! You're our guy, you hang on! Sand rushes into his mouth. It clings to his teeth, his dry gums. The leading man's chest and legs are slapping against the desert floor in a quick, silent rhythm. He doesn't feel pain. Sand has blocked his nostrils, his throat, and the air is gone. He leaves his body and observes himself being dragged by a dying horse.

The leading man thinks he sees his third wife, his blond-haired, blue-eyed third wife, the actress, the one he loved more than his own breath. He remembers the date of the Friday morning phone call: January 16, 1942. He was at their San Fernando ranch. What he remembers next is being thirty miles from Las Vegas and smelling the oily fire and smoke and trying to climb the goddamn mountain. People held him and patted his arm and said, Okay, okay, shhh, quiet down now. They didn't get it. All he wanted to do was pull what was left of her from the airplane.

May 1962
Los Angeles

Dr. Woetzel is listening to N. J. talk about her leading man. It's the last fifteen minutes of their session. Afternoon sunlight cuts a vivid yellow path through the office. The warmth of the room and N. J.'s Chanel has left the doctor fighting sleep. Maybe he wanted to die, N. J. says. You know, like a suicide you keep from yourself. People do that, don't they? Keep it from themselves? The sunlight reveals her crossed legs and her ruby red shoes. N. J. says, I saw everything, the way that horse dragged him, how he held on. He never got up. His heart burst or something, I don't know. I thought he'd fainted from the heat. N. J. is mostly in the shadows, her Oleg Cassini black linen suit, her small, thin fingers and the red nail polish that matches her shoes.

Do you do that? Dr. Woetzel says in a soft voice. Do you keep such things from yourself? Those times when you drank too much and took too many Nembutal, did you think it was only a mistake, did you keep it from yourself? Then Dr. Woetzel looks down at N. J.'s ruby red shoes and says, I think you did. Am I wrong? Please, feel free to tell me if I'm wrong.

N. J. stares at Dr. Woetzel and blinks. Her fingers begin touching the back of her hair, playing with the loose platinum ends. I wouldn't do that, N. J. says. I know I haven't paid attention to my medication and my drinking in the past. But I wouldn't do that. I'd never kill myself for anybody.

The room is so warm; the Chanel, so sweet and thick. Dr. Woetzel wants to drift away, perhaps take a nap for a minute or two. She always gets sleepy when something isn't right, when something isn't making sense. Memories start to unfold, the distant and familiar gunfire of the SS women. The prisoners who say, Aren't you supposed to help sick people get better? How can you call yourself a doctor? Dr. Woetzel doesn't have that answer. There are mornings she questions why God has spared her and let the others die. She knows when things aren't right. It's a gift.

Jennifer Hurley

PIPES

Two summers ago David Wood showed up at my apartment with seventeen pipes and a picnic basket. We walked to the park and spread out a blanket, hoped for sun, and looked up at the clouds and, finally, after eating cold sandwiches with the lettuce falling out of them, we packed up our things and left.

Back in my apartment, the sun was brilliant, slicing through the blinds, gilding the beige silk fabric of the couch. David kneeled on the floor and began taking out his pipes. He told me about each one of them, where he found them and how old they were, and what type of tobacco was best to smoke in them. The last one he brought out from the bag was a gift: a curved three-ounce piece of wood, honey-colored, glossy enough to offer a foggy glimpse of my own eye.

He taught me how to fill the pipe and light it with a special lighter that made the flame tilt sideways, and how to suck on the tip until I tasted the woolly flavor of the smoke. Stretched out on the couch, we puffed and blew—smoke filled the room, drifted out the opened window. When my flame went out, he taught me how to stamp down the tobacco using a miniature silver foot and to puff quickly until specks of orange flared up inside.

The pipes lasted a long while, through two glasses of dark German beer, but it was impossible to know what time it was and whether the sun angling through the blinds, sending dust motes spiraling through space, was morning sun or afternoon sun.

It was the only time I ever used the pipe. Months later, when I saw David on campus and we were strangers again, he said he had stopped smoking. The tobacco was making him dizzy and, besides, there was no place to smoke anymore. He said he had given away all his pipes. Now he was spending his money on cuff links and tea.

The pipe in its flannel case has ended up in my desk drawer next to a can of shredded Virginia tobacco that has probably gone stale. When I lived in Virginia, many years ago, I used to see strips of tobacco hanging from the rafters of open barns in late fall. I never thought then about how tobacco was harvested, hung, dried, shredded, packed and sealed into cans, then shipped across the country or even further. Soon I will have to throw my can away because it is making my stationery smell strange, and people keep asking me if I am back to smoking again.

If I did go back, I would want the kind of life that would allow for a pipe. Sluggish afternoons, a leather chair with cracks in it, a deck of cards with the backing nearly worn off. Not a cigarette kind of life, the desperate trips outdoors in freezing weather, a few quick sucks, the rest discarded.

Pipes are grandfatherly things, but I know hardly anyone with a grandfather anymore; all of them have died, some of them from the muck of tobacco in their lungs, and their pipes have taken up residence in antique shops, stuffed in drawers that only a few people ever try to open. Maybe it's better that the pipes stay there. Pipes don't fit in nowadays. They are like handwritten letters—charming, quaint, but ultimately serving no real purpose except to nudge us into daydreams of the past, how things must have been better then, forgetting for a moment that the things we carry now also fade, ever so gradually, into relics themselves.

Mairéad Byrne

THE PRESSURE

This evening I cleaned the fridge. The pressure. You know when you have all the milk cartons out. Oh! I know it's November. But unseasonably warm, right. The pressure. The pressure. It was horrendous. It was hellish. I went at it like the devil. Like a giant *Energizer* bunny. *Brrrrrrrrrrrrrrrrrrrrrrrrrrrrr!* My attack was kinda like a sander, kinda like a drill, kinda like a chainsaw. *Out, out, everything out! Hands over heads! Lay down your weapons!! Put your weapons down!!!!* A jar of *Newman's Own* (garlic & peppers) tried to hide out at the back—sorta like the ending of *Butch Cassidy*—but we forked it out, along with a colony of yogurt occupying the zone. Rooted them out screaming. Brie! Ham! Pickles! You name it. Things crawling everywhere, trying to burrow into the corners of the crisper. There was a hardened Parmesan hanging onto the door. You're never too old to fight. Then there they all were—huddled on the counter-top. What a crew. Half of them rotten. Scared. Some of them just kids. But still: past their sell-by date. In some cases grievously past. They had to go. Over the top. One after another— I had lined up the garbage can—*GO! GO! GO!* Have you ever seen a pint of half-and-half quaking, man? How about 3 chocolate macaroons? They were *white!* [CLEARS THROAT] Sure, there were items I felt sorry for. I'm human. I felt sick for them. But that's life. It's *Thanksgiving*, man. We're moving the new guys in.

R. Kimm

wie gesagt: "Anredsam"

Die Huehnen machen
laute boese Geraeusche
typisch wie die laute
Vogeln die sind

Etwas bewegt sich
im Rasen draeben.

Du bist so
"a schaine."

"like the fella says
—'speakable'"

The chickens make
lots of noise like
the loud birds
they are.

Something is mov-
ing in the grass.

You're such
a cutie.

—Translated from the German by the author

Gloria Garfunkel

Birds of Prayer

Christmas carols clamored inside Grace's head. For school friends, Santa Claus was coming to town. But for Grace, the Chicken Killer from Brooklyn was arriving at any minute by train with his satchel full of death tools.

"To slay our chickens whether naughty or nice," she thought from the back seat of the Chevy her grandfather was driving slowly through the snow on chained tires to the train station in December 1959. "And there is nothing I can do to stop him."

"You are such a quick learner, Gittikahh," Zeidika remarked to his eight-year-old granddaughter in the rearview mirror. "I can't believe you are so strong. You lifted that heavy rooster by yourself. You are as careful at collecting eggs as my best workers. You are the fastest on the whole farm at grading eggs with none breaking. I am so proud of you."

"I would rather do any of those chores than go to school or help Mommy around the house," Grace replied. Zeidika laughed with his soothing breath of garlic cloves rubbed on *matza* each morning, just like his father back in Hungary and his grandfather before him.

Zeidika parked under a streetlamp, snow falling, Christmas lights blinking, dusk deepening. Grace noticed that the train station was built of the same looming rocks as the church beside it, as if they had erupted together from the ground and would last forever. Three churches were visible from the car. Each sparkling tree outdid the other. Each flood-lit manger contained a life-size baby Jesus surrounded by adoring grown-ups and farm animals.

Grace huddled under a blanket in the back seat, shivering, humming *Come all Ye Faithful*, her secretly favorite Christmas carol that she belted out loudly in school chorus. Zeidika stomped around outside. Grace counted falling snowflakes, feathery Stars of David that she believed parachuted homesick Jewish souls back to earth.

"Is that what six million looks like?" she wondered. She easily grasped the six part, her sister Lucy's age, two years younger than Grace, the six symmetrical points of a Jewish star and of snow crystals. But six standing like a Gestapo guard in front of six hollow zeroes? Grace could be swallowed by the pain-rays that oozed like radioactivity from her parents' concentration camp wounds. An avalanche of absence had buried most of her parents' families at the bottom of a snow-globe universe cupped in the hands of an unreliable God.

"One day we lived in our safe little world, and the next day everything was gone," they repeated like a prayer. Grace was constantly aware, both during the day and in her nightmares, that it could happen again.

She wiped condensation with her pink bunny mittens to glimpse from the window the blurry fanfare of lights. Two weeks until Christmas. Two days until Hanukah. They were the only Jewish family in Greenhouse Station, New Jersey.

"Our so-called Miracle of Lights is based on some puny olive oil staying lit for eight days instead of one," Grace contemplated. "Compared to Passover's Ten Amazing Plagues and a split Red Sea, God's power seems to be weakening over time. Maybe He is getting old, or wearing down like a battery."

His miracles had certainly petered out by the time her parents needed them. Grace's fat book of fairy tales had more impressive rescue missions than God's Hanukah light trick. Thumbelina and her rescue bird. The Snow Queen in her palace of ice lit up by the Aurora Borealis, where little frozen Kay frolicked with ice cubes, unaware that he was dead. He kept trying to form the word "eternity" to break his spell, until he was finally resurrected by the hot tears of his best friend, Gerda. Of course Hansel and Gretel, with their ultimate rescue from the oven of an evil witch, pushing her inside instead. What possible excuse did All-Mighty God have for refusing to help the children in Grace's family locked in cattle trains and gas chambers, then burned in ovens? Did He spin a *dreidle* like her family did on Hanukah to randomly determine everyone's fate?

Just then, a Hasidic Jew appeared out of nowhere, like Elijah the Prophet, waiting under the station's arch. Zeidika lumbered over to greet the camouflaged killer.

"Hired like a Nazi to slaughter dozens of our chickens with some ritual that makes them kosher," thought Grace, wondering how she might rescue the birds.

In overalls, earflaps and muddy work boots, Zeidika blended with the townspeople. But in his long black coat that tied like a bathrobe, the Hasid stood out like a neon kosher sign blazing from a butcher shop in Brooklyn. His flat hat, a fur-trimmed *streimel*, lay on his head like a platter of dead minks, the man's corkscrew side-locks dangling like pigtails.

As the men approached, Grace slid down the seat, hoping no classmates would spot her. In Miss Witherspoon's third grade class at Hummingbird County Public Elementary School, Grace's social goal was invisibility, the name on her birth certificate a camouflage for the Gittel she really was with family.

At the start of each school day, Grace bowed her head over clasped hands, reciting the Lord's Prayer with everyone else. She rehearsed as a snowflake dancing around the Christ child for Christmas pageants her parents never allowed her to attend. Her life might someday depend on such stealth, as it once had for her cousin Shifra, ten years older than Grace, the daughter of her father's brother, Mischa.

Shifra had pretended to be a Christian woman's daughter in Poland for four years, from the time she was three until she was seven. Edie changed Shifra's name to Marianna, and doted on her, never expecting Shifra's family to return. But when Uncle Mischa appeared at Edie's door after the war, Marianna hardly recognized the skinny stranger. He kept calling her Shifra and saying that her real mother and siblings were dead and that he was her father. Shifra clung to Edie, the only parent she knew. Edie, still single, offered to marry widowed Uncle Mischa, just to keep her Marianna, but he refused because of Edie's Christianity. Uncle Mischa left with sobbing Marianna, now

Shifra, to a refugee camp in Germany, where he ended up marrying oily Aunt Rivka, who reeked of sweat and sarcasm. Shifra never again saw the woman who had saved her life while all her relatives and play-mates were dying.

So Grace memorized Christian beliefs just in case it might happen again, even though everyone already knew she was Jewish because of all the school she missed for Jewish holidays. She cross-examined classmates about the finer points of Christianity like Perry Mason, the TV lawyer, questioning witnesses to a crime. In the girls' room and on the playground she relentlessly instigated religious debates. To her parents, *Goyim* were all the same. But Grace had uncovered dissent among the sects, though they all agreed that Jews were outcasts.

One day on the playground, Kelly Ann O'Reilly, Grace's under-cover catechism instructor, said "I'm sorry to tell you that Jews are Christ-Killers, and though I don't blame you personally, you really should think about converting to Catholicism to avoid going to Hell."

Know-it-all Harold Slater, the principal's son, hanging upside-down from the nearby monkey bars, scoffed, "You're a Catholic, Kelly Ann? My dad says you're both going to Hell."

Nancy Smith, usually very shy, piped up, "I'm Episcopalian, but I don't even believe in Hell. I mean, who's ever come back with proof? That's what Grammy Maggie says."

It was 1959 and Grace already knew that there did indeed exist a Hell on Earth. She was much more worried about its resurrection than any Biblical Hell.

Zeidika guided the Hasid to the front seat, heaving the stranger's satchel into the back like a carcass.

"Gittikah, this is Mr. Unger," Zeidika said, starting the car.

"The chicken killer?" she asked.

"The *shochet*," Mr. Unger corrected, slashing the word in half with that gurgling, Yiddish throat sound. "To make your chickens kosher. Jews are very particular. No birds of prey. No *tsaar baaley chaim*, suffering to the animal. I have a very sharp knife and a very quick hand. Without me, you would have nothing to eat. Just your spinach."

"I could live on spinach if I had to," Grace thought. In fact, she felt guilty every time she ate chicken, trying hard not to think of its bones as the actual wings and legs of one of the silky creatures she gently tended, held, and petted whenever she had a chance.

Mr. Unger complained to Zeidika in Yiddish about the train transfers from Brooklyn. Grace's father rode trains for hours every day to his job in the fur district of Manhattan and never complained. Zeidika ran the farm instead of working in a gas station like he had in the Bronx, before they all purchased the farm. Grace was just a baby then, with no city memories.

She cringed beside Mr. Unger's satchel. Though evil, it resembled Dr. Lyons' leather bag brought on house calls to defend life from germs, which Grace pictured as microscopic German soldiers. Mr. Unger's clothes exuded the mothball vapors one would expect from a close associate of the Angel of Death. Grace opened the window a slit for fresh air. Apparently, Jews could eat only innocent animals, not predators.

"Perhaps so we can absorb the animal's peaceful nature," Grace thought, remembering how her family foisted their sins upon a squawking chicken Zeidika swung over their heads before slaughtering it for Yom Kippur.

"We must have exchanged our sins for its innocence then too," she reasoned. Timid and flightless, chickens were perfect prey. They were startled by car horns, even creaking doors. Whenever Grace collected eggs, she moved in slow motion, as if under water. Otherwise chickens would explode in a burst of dust and feathers, with broken eggs everywhere.

"How can you know for sure what chickens are feeling?" Grace asked Mr. Unger, who ignored her. Grace's parents seemed unable to tell what even she was feeling. So how could rabbis be certain that a quick slit of the throat was less painful than a blow to the head, a shotgun blast, a heave into an oven or even breathing poison gas? She had plugged her ears with her fingers while running out of the house when her baby brother had shrieked as the *mohel*, a sort of *shochet* in reverse, welcomed the boy to the pain of Jewish life by slicing off a piece of his penis.

"Are kosher chickens Jewish once they're dead?" Grace tried again. But Mr. Unger blabbered over her words. He reminded her of God the Unmerciful, the trickster, saving Isaac from sacrifice by his father Abraham, yet slaughtering millions of Isaac's descendants down the line of history. To people who did not make the connection, God remained merciful and popular. But Grace wasn't fooled.

"These are my chosen people," her right bunny mitten bragged to the Satchel of Doom. "*Shochet* Hitler, I am God. I will not save any of the Jews I select for you. Guaranteed."

"What did you say, Gittikah?" called Zeidika.

"Nothing, just playing," she replied, silencing the mitten-mouth of God in her lap.

"She has a big imagination, that one," boasted Zeidika. Mr. Unger launched into bragging about his ten pious children, "nine of whom, thanks to *Hashem*, are *boychiks*."

"Thanks to Hashem, I'm a girl," Grace mumbled, happy that she had fewer religious obligations than males. And then her left mitten narrator continued, "So even though Zeidika's mother, Clairel, and wife, Gittel, and his four youngest children had prayed for God to pluck them from their plight like the giant bird who had saved tiny Thumbelina from her rodent captors, even though they held their hopes and breaths until they could hold them no longer, God kept his promise to Hitler. No one lived happily ever after. Hardly anyone lived at all. The end."

Zeidika glanced back at his granddaughter for a moment. She knew those translucent blue eyes as both loving and remote, warm like the sun but frozen like ice. Zeidika saw her filtered through the overlapping ghosts of his missing children. She wished she could thaw his grief, bring him more fully into their shared present. She believed his heart to be encased in the icy grip of the Snow Queen, and that all he needed to do was cry for them all, something he never did, not one tear that she ever heard of. Even her mother had said so.

"He had to be strong for everybody," her mother had said.

The Snow Queen was one of Grace's favorite tales in the book she had won in a school spelling bee. It was as large as her father's volumes of the Talmud with print as tiny and which she studied as fervently, each story accompanied by a detailed illustration. From it, she learned that tears could cure a frozen heart.

Snow was falling heavily, feathery flakes, like the gigantic chickens in her book pulling the little boy Kay behind the Snow Queen's sled, approaching her Palace of Death in the distance.

Zeidika drove slowly, windshield wipers swaying like her piano lesson metronome, reminding her of the index finger of the Nazi guard who greeted Grace's parents at the entrance to Auschwitz, pointing this way and that, mechanically sorting family members like laundry, without skipping a beat.

"This way to life, that way to death. We didn't know it at the time, but that was what it meant." Her parents both repeated this frequently, each time their pupils becoming bottomless black holes, as they waved a forefinger like a hypnotist's pendulum, trying to absorb the arbitrariness of their families' slaughter and their own survival.

Grace was carsick by the time they veered into the barely visible dirt road of Faraway Farm, a name reflecting the grown-ups' longing for what they all referred to as Home, back in Hungary and Poland, as if where they lived now, the only home Grace knew, was not really home to them at all. Her parents' real homes were occupied by thieves. Their beloved families existed backwards in time.

The threesome entered Zeidika's half of their two-family farmhouse. Grace's step-grandmother, Magda, appeared dressed up, her lips blood red, her coal hair tied back with a scarlet kerchief, tendrils curling around her flushed face. She wore a frilly hot-pink apron crawling with red roses over a purple silk dress. Her stocking seams shot straight up the back of her legs from her high-heeled white-feathery slippers.

"Mr. Unger, come in! Welcome to our poor farmhouse," Magda exclaimed. He glanced uncertainly at Zeidika who gestured him on. They followed Magda's prancing figure into her kitchen where Hungarian delicacies had been bubbling all day.

"Sit. Gittikah, have some of my delicious sauerkraut and potato soup. I made it especially for you."

The three sat around the kitchen table while Magda bustled about, mesmerizing the *Shochet* by stuffing his mouth for the rest of the evening. Stranded in their farmhouse, this former Budapest socialite was thrilled to have a new audience for her concoctions, especially a visitor about to slaughter several months' worth of poultry for her freezer. Magda's head bobbed over wooden spoons she dipped into broths, stirring and tasting, steam billowing, fogging every window. She sang Yiddish and Hungarian folk songs, swinging her hips from side to side.

Magda and Grace's mother, Ilona, both cooked ferociously, as both had once starved. Often not on speaking terms, they would hand Grace measuring cups, instructing her to ask the other to borrow sugar, oil, flour, or salt. Regardless of the weather, Grace shuttled along the concrete path linking their separate entrances to the same farm-house, never leaving either kitchen without a taste of the most recent production. While Magda's cooking was tempestuous and peppery, Ilona's was soothing and rich. Both artfully balanced sweet and sour, cinnamon and cloves, caraway and garlic, salt and paprika, temporarily conjuring the spirits of the dead with their challahs, strudels, kishkas, stuffed cabbages, and stews, as if just the right combination of ingredients could transport them all back to a time before anyone realized how unsafe life could be. Though Grace complimented both equally, Magda relentlessly informed visitors that Grace loved her cooking the best.

"Time for bed, Gittikah," Ilona called through the screen of their heated closed-in porch that was used mostly for their frequent over-flow of relatives from Brooklyn.

"Finish your sauerkraut soup," Magda chided. Grace noticed some goulash stuck to Mr. Unger's beard.

"I have to go," Grace said, passing the loyalty test in favor of her mother. Zeidika and Grace kissed each other. Magda presented her powdered cheek.

"Good-bye Mr. Unger," Grace said. He waved her off like a fly, his cheeks stuffed like a chipmunk's.

"She loves my cooking better than her own mother's," Grace heard Magda say as she slammed the door.

Grace meandered in the fresh snow of the front yard, still counting flakes falling in the light outside her porch.

"Mommy, how come you and Magda never talk to each other?" Grace asked as she peeled off her snowy boots in the doorway.

"She said something bad about you as a baby," her mother replied, her back to Grace while washing dishes.

"What was it?"

Ilona paused mid-scrub to lean on the sink. Though she wore a plain, faded housedress and came from a poor village on the opposite side of Hungary from glamorous Budapest, Grace noticed the porcelain translucence of her ivory skin that everyone remarked on, so beautiful compared with the floury coarseness of Magda's pampered face.

"I don't remember, but I know it was bad. Now get ready for bed."

Grace had trouble thinking of baby insults sufficient to explain their longstanding rift. Her mother compared Magda's "rotten nature" to the "sweet nature" of her own mother, Gittel. Grace therefore suspected that baby insults were a cover story. Just being alive while Gittel was dead was likely Magda's most unforgivable sin.

"How many were there?" Grace asked her mother, as they checked on her sleeping baby brother, Jake, and her little sister, Lucy.

"Such *zeekeits*. I could eat them up," her mother whispered, kissing each of their cheeks. "What did you ask?"

"What were their ages?" Grace persisted. "What were their names?"

As she did most nights, Ilona recited her siblings' names and ages the last time she saw them, when she was sixteen. And just as always, as she uttered the syllables, they transformed into sparks charging the air, casting a spell, so that Grace could not grab the answers before they evaporated like zeroes. Nevertheless, she felt compelled to ask again and again for the identities of those who had flickered briefly on earth before her, like fireflies. She forgot what her mother said no matter how many times they repeated this ritual like a prayer every night. Grace's mother seemed entranced by this incantation between waking and sleeping, to punctuate each day. Together they evoked invisible gravestones in the puffs of air and sounds between them, in a world with no other markers of those fleeting lives.

The only name Grace ever remembered was that of Gittel, her grandmother, because it was given to her. She embodied Gittel in the world of the living, just as Grace's Yiddish name connected her to the land of the dead. She felt her grandmother watching over her with compassion, although helpless to intervene on her behalf under the icy scrutiny of stern God Almighty, as Gittel had been powerless to rescue her own four little ones huddling around her like ducklings in the gas chamber.

As Ilona recited the names, she tearfully called Grace "Mameleh," Little Mother, which confused the child. Were those Grace's siblings who had died? Grace's own mother rather than grandmother? Competent Ilona seemed so fragile then, between day and night. Carrying her grandmother's name, Grace wished she could protect her daughter-like mother from past harm as if she were her own child, as if time could zigzag back and forth.

Only Zeidika never seemed to weaken, though it was his wife and children who had been murdered. Both Grace's parents were irritable, volatile at times, but Zeidika, her only living grandparent, was their steady compass, calming her parents when they lost their patience with their children and placating his often-shrieking wife, Magda, reliably centering them all.

That evening, the *Shochet* snored on a pull-out couch in Zeidika's cozy closed-in porch. The next morning, he and Zeidika awoke before dawn, snaking around their arms the leather straps of *tefillin* attached to little prayer cubes perched on top of their foreheads and hands. Each draped over his shoulders and head a white *tallis* with fringes hanging like the spread-out wings of a giant bird. They recited the morning prayers that long ago replaced animal sacrifice in Jewish ritual. Then, in his rickety truck, Zeidika drove the executioner up to the coops to begin a long day of stooping in a white blood-stained robe over surgically precise throat-slashing.

After breakfast, Grace badgered her mother into letting her help for the day, leaving Lucy and Jake with their babysitter to watch cartoons. School was closed for a snow day, so Ilona relented. Together, mother and daughter trudged to the coops, just as flurries began again. Walking down the hill from the house to the dirt road, they passed the snow-covered vegetable garden and the skinny wooden shed that exuded the charred aroma of smoked geese and ducks against an impenetrable gray sky. On the road climbing up towards the coops, Mother walked along the tire tracks, but Grace stumbled through fresh snow higher than the tops of her red boots. They passed the bright yellow gasoline pump for fueling the tractor, the bare weeping willow hanging over the frozen frog creek, the Concord grape arbor the children picked clean every fall and the hump of snow-covered sand hill Grace pretended was a desert every summer. Up ahead, just outside a long cinder block building called the Hatchery, where Zeidika warmed eggs in incubators and nurtured baby birds every spring, Grace could see the winter slaughter had begun, half-way between her house and four large coops of squawking chickens.

Approaching the carnage, Grace stretched her neck, wrapped in an itchy woolen scarf, to observe from a safe distance, wondering how she might save even one chicken. Ilona reported to Zeidika that Magda had a headache "as usual" and was lying down "with an aspirin" before joining them. Mosey, their head farm worker, a black man who had worked alongside Zeidika for as long as Grace could remember, hauled and stacked wooden cages like tiny enclosed cribs, each crowded with screeching birds.

"Steer clear, Kitty Kat, or they'll mistake you for a chicken," shouted Mosey.

"You're joking," Grace replied.

"Me, joke? You got me mixed up perhaps with some other gentleman?"

"Yes, you told me I'll sleep in the bungalow with the freezers next summer."

"That's no joke. You most surely will, my dear. Leavin' space for a cot just your size when we finish in the spring."

"Mommy says that's not true."

"Just you wait, come summer, who's tellin' you the truth, honey."

Zeidika, meanwhile, assisted the *shochet* the way Mother often helped Dr. Lyons immobilize Grace for penicillin shots. Zeidika firmly restrained each bird through the procedure, gently rubbing their heads while softly singing Hungarian lullabies. He could hypnotize them into limpness before they were killed.

Mr. Unger recited Hebrew blessings, maneuvering a razor-sharp knife with his corpse-white hand so fast that Grace could not perceive the moment of death, though she monitored each flick of the wrist and alarming spurt of blood that stained the snow below in seeping redness.

The flurries intensified. Snow fell on blood, blood on snow, like Snow White's lips, red as blood, and skin, white as snow and silky chicken feathers. Grace thought of the sharp pain of paper cuts and remembered the shock of once stepping on broken glass, something like what the chickens must feel when the knife parted their necks. The scene resembled a distant play in a tiny shaken snow globe that she felt suffocated inside, yet detachedly outside all at once. It was difficult to breathe, as if her lungs were confined in a crowded cage.

Mosey transported the limp birds by their legs, two birds in each hand, to the hatchery building with its high windows and bare bulbs hanging from rafters. There, he hoisted cadavers up and down from their hooks so Mother, a few of the other workers, and eventually Magda could pluck feathers and scrape guts over long metal table-tops resting on sawhorses, a process inexplicably referred to as "dressing the chickens." Hanging featherless by their tied-up stick legs, the lifeless fowl looked more to Grace like creatures in need of clothes and a burial than freezing and cooking.

Grace's palms dampened with sweat despite the cold. She scurried between the doomed living and the freshly dead, wondering how it felt to be suddenly headless, cold air blasting into one's neck. The crammed birds were frantic, but fear apparently did not count as suffering in *Kashrus* law. She could feel their terror permeate her body.

She imagined trying to herd them back into warm coops without chickens scampering in every direction and freezing to death. She remembered her parents' claim that in the hierarchy of suffering, these were just senseless animals, not sensitive humans. But like so much else they found comforting, this did not calm her at all, for she recalled them quoting Nazis who'd said the same things about Jews.

"Vermin, they called us. Our lives were cheap," she often heard.

Grace's intensifying panic triggered an even worse feeling of unreality. She hated this floaty, out-of-body feeling, colors brighter, hurting her eyes, for it made her feel like she was watching herself in a dream. And if so, where was she, Grace worried, in her waking life? Was she trapped in a bunk of blanket-less wooden slats in Auschwitz? Was she crowded in a dark stinking cattle car or awaiting slaughter in a gas chamber? Was she, in fact, a trapped chicken dreaming of flight?

To drown these concerns, Grace assigned herself the task of purging the concrete floor with a water hose. While the grown-ups toiled up to their elbows in blood, she directed a Red Sea to the drain in the slightly sunken middle of the room. Everyone splashed around in rubber boots, but while Grace shivered in her snowsuit, Mother and Magda perspired in light sweaters, yanking out feathers and slithery organs, washing corpses, then sprinkling them with giant salt crystals to draw out the blood which was banned for consumption under the tenets of *kashrus*.

The *shochet* shuffled to the bathroom. Grace dropped the hose and ran outside. His leather knife case rested on a stool. She removed her mittens to feel the soft leather pouch, then slowly slid out the knife. The blade's edge seemed thinner than paper. Grace held out her left hand, like Isaac's throat. She passed the blade lightly across the tip of her forefinger, parting her flesh like a chicken's neck. Out gushed blood, with no pain whatsoever, just a chill up the back of her neck. She dropped the knife and its pouch in the snow.

"Has anyone seen my knife?" the *shochet* boomed. Grace scampered back inside to hose off her hand. Mr. Unger located his knife in the snow and glanced in Grace's direction through the open door. The water numbed her finger, but as soon as she removed the flow, the finger poured blood. She ran to the bathroom and pressed the cut with wads of toilet paper. Mosey barged in.

"I knew you's the snoop fiddlin' with that butcher knife. Show me the damage."

He knelt to examine her finger.

"Cut your finger almost right off, Kitty Kat."

"Please don't tell my mother. She'll kill me."

"Maybe if you promise not to go touchin' more knives. I'm gonna bandage this up real tight so all the insides of your finger don't go fallin' out like chicken guts. But first, I gotta clean it with iodine to kill those germs. That's gonna sting plenty. So take a deep breath and think snow. Be glad you ain't no chicken."

The searing pain did make Grace glad that the chickens had all died quickly, before the pain set in. At least she now knew that their death was indeed painless. Mosey wrapped her finger tightly in layers of gauze and then round and round with white tape.

"You should scat down to the house and be watchin' cartoons with the other little kids, anyways, not messin' around with all these blood and guts. What's the matter with your folk? This ain't no place for no nosy-body little girl. Why these people let you up here in the first place?"

"I begged them."

"Oh, so I suppose if you pestered them to let you drive the tractor, they gonna say 'Here the keys, girl. Bye! Don't run over no geese.' This is crazy stuff, Kitty Kat. Jesus."

Grace pulled his jacket.

"Thank you, Mosey, for helping me."

"Real helpin' would be marchin' you right back down to that warm old farmhouse where you belong." He waved Grace away as if disgusted and went back to work. She wandered out of the bathroom, embarrassed that Mosey thought her family so strange. Mother stood square and sturdy, preoccupied with feather-plucking, her high cheekbones reddened, fluffy down caught among the black curls escaping from under her red-checkered kerchief. Never too close to her worked the regal Magda.

By the end of the day, plastic bags filled with chicken carcasses were ready for freezing. Both women's hands were chafed and scarlet from the combination of icy water, frigid winds, bucketsful of blood and giant crystals of kosher salt that came in bright red and yellow boxes, each emblazoned with a white Star of David.

At dusk, just before Zeidika drove the *shochet* back to town, he who had ignored Grace all day took her aside.

"You ask too many questions, little one. Have more faith in *Ha Kadosh Baruch Hu*. Rest your troubled thoughts with Him. He has His reasons for everything. Accept that you can never fully know those reasons. And as they say in America, curiosity killed the cat." He pinched her cheeks roughly and departed. She rubbed her stinging face with relief. The slaughter was over, for now.

By evening, the Hatchery was scoured and they were all exhausted, ready to return to the farmhouse. There, Grace's father would arrive even later from the shop in New York City, where he sewed mink coats and often brought home extra pieces to sew in the attic late into the night. Every penny he earned kept the farm going.

But before they emerged into the starlit night, Mother and Magda grilled some salted chicken livers held over a blow-torch clasped in a metal double-grid with a handle so it could be flipped over. The charred organs melted on their tongues like chocolate, quelling hunger pangs and completing a cycle of transforming creatures into sanctified food suitable for Jewish consumption, erasing all thoughts of suffering with sensations of eating pleasure, albeit incited by animal sacrifice.

"You take care, Kitty Kat," said Mosey, plunking Grace onto her mother's lap in the truck, next to Magda. As Zeidika drove back to the house, Mosey wiggled his left forefinger and winked. He lived in an apartment attached to the hatchery, with the three transient farm workers who never talked to Grace at all.

That night in bed, Grace mumbled the usual Hebrew prayers to placate God's wrath for another night of fitful sleep under his ogre finger pointing to life and death. Her head propped up on two goose down pillows, she gazed at her night-lit walls filled with crayon drawings of birds she had seen around the farm: Goldfinches, Cardinals, Orioles, Red-Winged Black Birds, Blue Jays, and of course the white geese and ducks with clipped wings that they raised by the thousands along the rivers and ponds all around the farm.

Grace pretended her walls were the sky and she was a giant, scanning the topography of her fluffy down comforter, a landscape of rolling hills and valleys. She thought of Thumbelina, trapped underground by two rodents harboring an apparently dead bird, whom she cared for anyway, luckily, because it turned out to be alive, just injured. Once healed, the bird whisked the girl from captivity. She envied the wings Thumbelina strapped on her back at the end of the story, so she could from that day forward rescue herself. She promised herself to add an impossibly flying chicken to her wall in the morning.

Grace fell asleep to the hum of her father's sewing machine in the attic. She had once tried to ask him how the minks were killed, if they had to die in a kosher way, and he had just answered, "Minks? They kill them in a gas chamber. Don't feel sorry for them. They're just vicious little weasels."

Grace fell asleep, dreaming that her bed had indeed moved to the freezer shed, as Mosey had predicted, pushed up against the fourth wall, the other three lined with coffin-shaped freezers storing dead birds and summer vegetables. The walls were built of blocks of ice like the Snow Queen's fortress, transparent, so she could see the greenish lights of the Aurora Borealis feathering up towards a blue moon. In the dream, Zeidika tucked her in, chanting a prayer that was vaguely familiar, though she could not decipher the meaning. But the rhythms formed a cadence that tumbled from his lips like diamonds, with crystals of salt or ice glittering in the corners of his eyes, sticking to his lashes.

Suddenly awakened in the dark, her heart pounding, Grace's nightgown drenched in sweat, she felt alarmed, feverish, and chilled. It hurt to swallow and her finger throbbed. She realized that it was she who was sobbing, not her grandfather. It was she who was chanting the suddenly-remembered names of Zeidika's murdered children. Aaron and Avraham, Hava and Lazer. Six was the number of Zeidika's children squashed into the sardine-can train to Auschwitz. These were the four youngest, tricked upon arrival into stripping for showers, their lives evaporating in poisonous fumes, leaving only the two oldest to survive, Grace's mother, Ilona, and her younger sister, Sara. Six was the age of the youngest girl, her Aunt Hava, Zeidika's precious Thumbelina, who could well have been Grace herself.

And so, shivering and burning up at once, Grace pretended she and Zeidika were cuddling in a feathery nest in the freezer shed with the bird corpses, while he finally sat *Shiva* for Gittel, Aaron, Avraham, Hava and Lazer. She wished that the frozen fortress around her grandfather's heart could melt as he heaved sobs, endless and deep, like the dying breaths of his children, a sea of tears to wash away all grief from Faraway Farm. But instead, only Grace cried, blindingly. Her throat ached so much she could barely breathe. I must be dying, she thought. Maybe that is why I suddenly remember the names. Maybe I am about to meet them all in Heaven.

She could see them there in Heaven, in an eternally bright Sunday, the summer of 1943, their last summer together. Her grandmother Gittel was bent over her elaborate herb garden, gathering sage and lavender for storing with winter blankets. Red and burgundy roses crawled all over the white clay house with its thatched roof. Zeidika's mother, Clairel, the one who had died on the train to Auschwitz, was picking parsley and carrots for soup. Lazer and Hava, the two youngest, their golden hair sparkling in the sunlight like twins, built ant houses with sticks. Sturdy sunflowers waved all around them in the warm breeze, dark centers ringed by light. Aaron, the Torah genius, put down the Biblical tract he was studying under a tree to help his crippled Aunt Rosa settle herself comfortably in the shade next to him. Then he read to her aloud. Avraham, Mr. Mischief, was chasing wary chickens, the very ones that had been slaughtered that day, trying to feed them some worms he had dug up. Aunt Sara and Grace's mother, Ilona, were teenagers, setting out with the horse and buggy to deliver seltzer for Zeidika's business while he was away temporarily at a labor camp. The cats crouched, then lept at butterflies, as Bodri, the big white farm dog with his long tangle of fur down to the ground sunned himself on the grass, belly up, nevertheless protecting the youngest two whom he shadowed.

Sobbing, Grace realized there was nothing she could do in this life to soothe Zeidika's sadness. Until he rejoined them after death, Zeidika's tears would remain frozen like that black-mirrored lake where the Snow Queen sat, right in the middle of her palace, watching little dead Kay try but fail to spell the magical word "eternity" with his blocks of ice. Grace tried to numb her aching finger, throat, and heart by spelling eternity over and over. But her perfect spelling skills held no magical powers to heal grief. She recognized the familiar symptoms of tonsillitis and wondered if her burning finger was rotting off, too.

If she did wake up the next morning, she would have to lie to her mother, saying she had cut her finger slicing bread. Mother would summon Dr. Lyons for a house call to aim yet another penicillin injection at Grace's behind, and maybe even one right through her finger. He loves to give shots, that man, Grace thought, always lying that it wouldn't hurt, before piercing her skin to eradicate germ soldiers.

Drifting back to sleep, Grace forgot the names again. As she struggled to remember, she tumbled back into her dream. There, she scouted for predators in the starlit night outside the freezer shed, this time fueled by an avian rage. She flapped her skinny arms, and lifted off the ground in her favorite pink flannel pajamas with feet, flying high into the sky. She could see the moonlit farm with its sleeping creatures and fields blanketed by snow, spread like a quilt below. She resolved that as long as God withheld miracles from his chosen children, she would do her best to protect her family and farm creatures, become a circling sentry hovering against a canopy of hollow darkness salted with countless Jewish stars yearning for their earthly homes. She would fly suspended between the lands of the dead and the living, longing for a God who loved her as fiercely as did Zeidika, a man who surely would have swooped out of the sky to rescue his littlest daughter and her three older brothers and their mother and grandmother, if only his All-Powerful God had granted him even the most fleeting miracle of flight.

Mark Neely

Four Flights

. . . others become angels at night, because no one has ever called them angels by day.

—Sigmund Freud

Most days are ordinary days, far from the flying we do in dreams. As I pay bills below the calendar's checkerboard, a sparrow kamikazes the patio door. I go out with a paper bag to clean it up. But every night the moon is sharper. I lie and listen to the trains, and count the stars bulging through my plaster walls. In my former sleep I floated over the maple heads, an undercover angel.

Because you are in Tokyo tonight, my charcoal shadow blows smoke across the porch boards. In your other language, you skip from subway to street, or press against a market wall to escape a storm. I'm a boy putting pennies on the train tracks, waiting. The real train blares and brings me back inside. In our bed after all, your eyelids leap with some red dream. The house fills up with air.

After the deaths, after months of bitter heat, a blast of air from Canada burns south like a comet until only a hint of its icy core remains in the wilted grass, and I think about the confidence of horses running down a hill, unsaddled, crazy with dust—their rumbling chests, their useless tossing manes, nostrils opened to the wind to the point of pain. Then I can fly again, the dead bird in my hand.

Here, the concussion of a southbound train cuts off our discussion. A sunlit stupor. You were trying to announce? Nothing left but embers of a forest blaze. The firefighters went away. The matinee ran all its shows of your hands—nervate, running out of tree time. Off to the annex then, to the prospects of panic, to experiments with different horsepowers, to mine and his and hers, but never ours.

Mary Cisper

Pandora Sets the Table

The scrape of spoon on metal, drawers opening.
On a good day the web holds, dinner on the stove.
Not so bad each one, the small beasts

loose in the world, tempered by distraction—
a daughter's gold hair, the purse she clutches with everything in it,
a son's clay village of dragons.

Still, a bruised door closes and opens.
The original lever, a day with clouds in it?
Last week the prayer flags stiffened with ice,

the red one tore, it was so heavy.
The pot stirred, fists under cover,
the six directions of powerlessness

against what is bought, what is given.
We shared a bed once.
My sister, did we wish for husbands

or a perfect knife, sufficiency? Which day to throw back,
which night to reel in to a white square of cloth?
The wash of games in the living room,

amaryllis in the window, its green thrust, adamant.
Today's rain a hard thread, it can't be cut.
Plates on the table, iron and chalk.

Stephen Gibson

A PETA Interpretation of a Gentlewoman in a Frieze Showing a Banquet

(Venice, July 2004)

One, limp, is held up by a noose; one, dressed, could be anything.
In the estate's background, amusing servants chase after a goose.

On her plate, the goose's liver bursts into delicious pâté
though she can hardly say how difficult it is for her

to know that dirty farmers force-feed them through funnels
until their bodies swell—well, that disgusts her.

Still, she won't stoop to berate her critics—she believes
doves are delicacies inside a cage and on a plate.

Net, strangle, club, shoot—they die so easily.
Birds that feed solely on berries taste like fruit.

Kathleen Hellen

The Girl Who Loved Mothra

A giant wing you know to be mechanical seems
real as faces in the front row lit by the
projection; faces barely seen until the screen
explodes with such artillery:
theater of war

where weapons don't prevail:
toy tanks and helicopters
dropping nets; U.S. artificial
lightning—useless in the fight
against bad sequels.

I bunker in the radiated glow; bug-eyed;
caterpillar eyebrows inching over glasses pushed up
to inspect the mutant wing:
a shield; a wound;
protecting;

a fan unfolding to adopt the offspring of
this unloved world; this monstrous egg
I loved; this prodigy of wind, big-
hearted aberration hatching
twins of you and me.

Kathleen Hellen

Homage to My Mother's Bath

I did not think it strange to see her naked
breasts; the scar where I was born
I did not think it foreign

when at ten (the Others, round-eyed children
laughing, who assumed the bath
a private thing
were Shocked?
Amused? thinking
how perverse, how public)
I was steeped in her beliefs

The two of us like dolls
the One inside
the Other
legs inside of legs
inside the tub
mine inside the greater
body of her influence

I liked it when she scrubbed; I shined
I liked it when she washed my hair; shampooed
the two great horns releasing
demons; like

dust the ginko gives up after rain
like rain the clouds release
How could they know?
I loved the slippery pearls of soap

diminishing;

the rinse
delicious as green tea?
I did not think it private, strange.

Kathleen Hellen

Tojo Eats the Stones of His Defeat

My mother's childlike hand
has printed "your dad"
on the back of the photo,
corresponding to the sepia-tone
figure of my father
in the foreground
looking down over wire rims
at a desk stacked with papers;
      slightly to the right, she writes:
              The Defense Attorney Mr. Blewitt;
        and below him,
              The Japanese Attorney Dr. Kiyose,
              who later became prime minister.
It is 1948. My father in the photo translates;
Mr. Blewitt reads from the pages of a document
not confession, not surrender.

Tojo stripped of medals at the top;
a nation's uniform belief
in earphones, behind
the stand of microphones;
flanked by anonymous guards;
the eyes behind the round-rim glasses piercing
through the tint, as if to say:
three thousand years before you
we were cultivating silk;
three thousand years from now
we will be crafting swords with blades turned out.

His smile, reserved—a smirk?
As if it was absurd. The war is never over,
never lost over a wound so near the heart:
From then to now;
from shogunate to these on trial:
from Tokyo's young lions to Meiji, me:
How does a country lose its face?
Become another place?
How does my father translate
generations in disgrace?

The maps we know only as maps—
China and Manchuria
the ABCD line—
become an alphabet of grief.
The photos we complete
when we look into the past;
know defeat; repeat it; serve up
shame like stones to eat
for everyone left hungry.

The war the war the war is never over.

Interview: Elyse Fenton

Elyse Fenton is an MFA student in poetry at the University of Oregon in Eugene. She has published poems in *Hubbub* and *Salamander*, and an essay on atrocity in *The Northwest Review*. Her husband returned safely from Iraq in November.

What sort of poem (in terms of subject matter, plot, theme) have you promised yourself you would never write?

Sometime in college I decided I would never again use the first person in a poem. That lasted about a week.

What bit of advice do you wish someone had told you when you first began your vocation as a writer?

A paper copy does not consist of adequate back-up.

Can you tell something about the origin of your poems, how they were written, where and what might have influenced them?

All of my poems in this journal come from my experience over the last year as the wife of an Army medic deployed in Iraq, and the continuous struggle to come to terms with the personal, poetic, and political ramifications of this reality. These poems spring from the groggy breathlessness of middle-of-the-night phone calls, from distance and desire, from a prolonged sense of dailiness-on-the-edge-of-destruction.

"Planting" comes from a day planting, yes, tomatoes, at a farm here in Oregon, a few days after my husband was involved in a bombing in Baghdad. I had been reading about the workings of elegy and the perceived impossibility of consolation in contemporary poetry the night before, and, fingers deep in the dirt, I couldn't shake the feeling that my concern for the leggy seedlings might, unsurprisingly, be displaced. "Planting" seemed to be the closest thing to consolation I could offer both Peenesh and myself. I'm pleased to say that the tomatoes (and, of course, my husband) did in fact survive.

How'd you get to be, you know, the way you are?

I come from Scrabble people.

Who are some of your most formative teachers?

In second or third grade, we had a Writers-in-the-Schools program, and the poet who came to our classroom, Judith Steinberg, brought a paper bag of rocks and seashells for us to observe and write about. I liked rocks a lot, especially with the new awareness that they had a place in the third grade literary canon. Soon after, I loved poetry.

What must you do before you can sit down to write?

Put on my gloves. My room gets pretty cold in the mornings.

What's your cure for writer's block or getting stuck in a story?

There's a series of running trails by my house, with various loops and connectors. When I'm stuck on a poem, I often go for a run. I get stuck enough that I've designated a few of the different loops for different problems I'm having. There's the Word-Finding loop, the

Thematic Problem hill sprint, and the Maybe I Should Just Scrap It butte climb.

What unique element or life experience do you bring to your writing that sets you apart from other writers?

I don't want to be the "war poet." I really don't. I struggle with the unfortunate belief that only those directly involved in the war garner the kind of street-cred that produces an "authentic" experience . . . At the same time, I realize that the experience of being a poet in an MFA program in a liberal town in the Northwest and having an active-duty soldier for a husband is unique, and has instilled in me an urgency that's been at the heart of, well, my heart, as well as my creative process, since before my husband left for Iraq.

When did you first begin to identify yourself as a writer?

I guess I've always had a sense of myself as a writer (my mother generously transcribed poems I spoke to her at age four) but it became more of a desirable title sometime in high school on the east coast, when I got the idea that poets either moved to the Pacific Northwest, or spontaneously generated there. Poetry, I figured not altogether illogically, was the ticket West.

Elyse Fenton

Love in Wartime (I)

Because there are seven-thousand miles
of earth & sky between us. Because

these lines are made of wind & fired
particles. Because at any moment the hard dust
beneath your feet could breach like a cleft
in meaning, could erupt into a sifting
cloud of brick & metal-riven bone

I have to believe in more than *signifiers*—

that the world cannot be deconstructed
by the word alone. That language is not
an uncoupling dance or the sparkless grinding
of meaning's worn flint, a caravan of phosphorous
tails burning up the breathable air.

When I say *you* I have to mean
not some signified presence, not
the striking of the same spent tinder

but your mouth & its live wetness, your tongue
& its intimate knowledge of flesh.

Elyse Fenton

Word from the Front

His voice over the wind-strafed line
      drops its familiar tone to answer
yes, we did a corkscrew landing down
      into the lit-up city, and I'm nodding

on my end, a little pleased by my own
      insider's knowledge of the way
planes avert danger by spiraling
      deep into the coned center of sky

deemed safe and I can't help but savor
      the sound of the word—shot tracer round
of pronunciation—and the image—
      a plane *corkscrewing*

down into the verdant green
      neck of Baghdad's bottle-glass night, so that
I don't yet register the casual solemnity
      of newscaster banter

falling like spent shells
      from both our mouths, nor am I
startled by the feigned evenness
      in my lover's tone, the way

he wrests the brief quaver
      from his voice like a pilot
pulling hard out of an engineless
      plummet, but only at the last minute

and with the cratered ground
      terrifyingly in sight—

Elyse Fenton

After the Blast

It happened again just now, one word
snagging like fabric on a barbed fence.

Concertina wire. You said: I didn't see the body
hung on *concertina* wire. This was after the blast.

After you had stood in the divot, both feet
in the dust's new mouth and found no one alive.

Just out of the shower, I imagine
a flake of soap crusting your dark jaw, the phone

cradled like a hand on your bare cheek.
I should say: love. I should say: go on.

But I'm stuck on *concertina*—
the accordion's deep inner coils, bellows,

lungful of air contracting like a body caught
in the agony of climax.

Graceless, before the ballooning rush
of air or sound. The battering release.

Elyse Fenton

GRATITUDE

When you tell me over the phone hours later
I can hear rotors scalping the tarmac-gray sky,
the lifted burden of your voice. Wreckage

was still smoldering on the airport road
when they delivered the soldier—*beyond recognition*,
seeing god's hands in the medevac's spun rotors—

to the station's gravel landing pad. How by the time
you arrived there were already hands fluttering
white flags of gauze against the ruptured scaffolding

of ribs, the glistening skull, and no skin left untended.
You were the one to sink the rubber catheter tube.
Listen, I love you more for holding the last good flesh

of that soldier's cock in your hands, for startling
his warm blood back to life. And I remember the way
that struck chord begins to shudder, the fierce heat

rising into the skin of my own sensate palms: that moment
just before we think the end will never come
and then the moment when it does.

Elyse Fenton

NOTES ON ATROCITY (BAGHDAD AID STATION)

Mid-conversation someone comes
looking for body bags. Medic,

love, I can hear you rummaging
the shelves, know the small fury

of your hands and the way
they used to settle, palms sinking

heavy bodies into mine. Outside
on my end, frost whittles the grass

to shards, the pear tree breathes
beneath a shroud of ice. When your voice

drifts above the shifted boxes, overheard,
it's washed in a tenderness I know

I'm not supposed to hear. As if
this were not the work of shrapnel—

not the body's wet rending, flesh
reduced to *matter*—but the litany

of an old field guide, the names
of wildflowers spoken out loud:

*ischium, basal ganglia, myelin-
sheathed endings.* Names for parts,

for all our flowering parts.

Elyse Fenton

Planting, Hayhurst Farm (June 5, 2006)

A week since the last bombing
brought you to your knees, since

the day you spent shoveling
human remains into a body bag

marked for home. I don't know
what to say. Neither of us has slept.

But today, planting peppers
on a farm in Oregon nowhere near

the war, I found myself mid-way
down a row, on all fours, hands

breaking open the rocky clods,
coaxing the flimsy necks to stand.

It felt like an exercise
in good faith—my fingers

blindly plunging, a brief tenderness
exacted on every stalk.

Some didn't make it through
our rough caging, some will never

bear fruit. I don't know
if this is even meant as consolation

but I want to tell you just how easy
it became to plant the thin bodies

in the ground, to mound up
the dense soil and move on.

Interview: Evan Morgan Williams

Evan Morgan Williams has published over twenty-five stories in such magazines as *Alaska Quarterly Review, Northwest Review, Blue Mesa Review,* and *Alimentum*. One of his stories was anthologized in *Best of the West: 5,* and two of his stories have been nominated for Pushcart Prizes. He has stories current or upcoming in *Alimentum, The Healing Muse, Ecotone,* and *You Are Here.*

What bit of advice do you wish someone had told you when you first began your vocation as a writer?

Be patient. You'll need years to get it right. Also, be patient with your readers; you'll need years to find them. These are the things I tell myself with every rejection slip. And, when I do get an acceptance, these things still ring true; my story was accepted because of my patient hard work, and my story was accepted because it found the right readers.

In my version of the world Gabriel García Márquez's *One Hundred Years of Solitude* would be more widely read than the *Da Vinci Code, Talk to Her* would win Best Picture at the Academy Awards and *Israel Kamakawiwo'ole* would play at least once a day from every radio in the world.

Can you tell something about the origin of your piece, how it was written, where, what might have influenced it?

The story has two origins: a dream from many years ago about a whale that beached during a minus tide, and a story I read in the first ever issue of *Glimmer Train*, called "Tinker." I don't remember the author's name, but the story is on my list of the Best Short Stories No One Bothers To Read Anymore.

Why do you think more good writing doesn't come out of prison where you would have so much time to write?

Writing requires community, whereas prison is cellular. On the other hand, maybe there is a ton of good writing in prison, but no one gets to read it. Maybe haiku gets tapped out on the pipes at night, but the echo doesn't last very long.

Who are some of your most formative teachers?

A big shout-out for the late Leonard Wallace Robinson. Also, Kent Nelson, Joanne Meschery, and Martha Geis. I can't exactly recall why each of them has been formative, but there they are. I remember that Leonard Robinson had four maxims, but I only recall two of them. Likewise Joanne Meschery had four maxims, but I only recall two. When I combine them together, I have a nice set of four again: seize form, know your own secret, elegance and efficiency of language, and generosity towards the reader.

What must you do before you can sit down to write?

I have to envision my time frame. How long will I have? How long until my little son wakes up from his nap? How long until my laptop battery fades? How long before we start dinner? How long can I keep my eyes open, because I'm so damn tired?

What's your cure for writer's block or getting stuck in a story?

Nothing overcomes a writer's block like a deadline. Whether it be for a class or for my writer's group, a deadline helps. It is also helpful to read fiction, then take up my pen and respond to what I've read. Last but not least, if one story isn't working, I try writing something else.

What do you think of the idea that more people write poetry or literary fiction than read it?

There's a wonderful section of Kundera's *Book of Laughter and Forgetting* where everyone is writing and no one is reading. I don't think that is reality, but if it were, some interesting possibilities could emerge: readers would be celebrated like rock stars. Their attention would be coveted, and they could name their terms. Drugs, women . . .

What is your most significant source of frustration as a writer? What do you love most about the act of writing?

Nothing is more frustrating than feeling like my stories are not being read with care. (I suppose that's beyond my control, so I should stop complaining). The thing I love the most about writing is the moment when a story takes on a presence more compelling than real life.

When did you first begin to identify yourself as a writer?

During my freshman year in college, a friend loaned me Barry Lopez's *River Notes*. It was a small collection of stories, and I read it several times in one night. Reading that book was an epiphany: I saw what I needed to do with my life.

Evan Morgan Williams

The Great Black Shape in the Shallow Water

I never understood why my mom did not fight back. She was as strong as ten Quihwa men, this at a time when feats of strength earned you the kind of regard money and looks get you nowadays. My dad was strong too, but unlike my mom he had never lifted a whale. He knew how to use his hands, though. Before he got his own boat, he hired onto some Finn's trawler out of Port Angeles, and being the only Indian he learned how to make a pretty good fist. I seen him punch through the ice on our cistern, a private show of anger that didn't earn him nothing in my book. My mom would never do that, and maybe that was the difference between them. I don't know, I was only twelve years old. I heard their fights muffled through a wall. I was too young to know there might be other stories not told.

What I know is this: one night many years ago, the waves left a Pacific right whale on the beach, a great heaving hump of black on the sand. You could see it from your porch in the morning, and a dozen families rang their bells to call everyone to the sand. The men were already out in their boats, and it fell to the women, children, and elders to lift the darn thing. It was like trying to lift a mountain off the earth itself. Well, my mom lumbered down the road, onto the beach, and she ·hoisted that whale's tail-fin over her shoulder and led us dragging the whale across the sand. We sang men's songs and found strength in our backs we didn't know we had. My mom's the one who got the whale back in the water, and by sundown when the men brought in their boats, the story had my mom carrying that whale all by herself. She was walking tall. She swaggered, she pushed up her sleeves to show off her biceps like a man. Children danced around her. She lifted me and my sister over her head, one laughing girl in each meaty hand, and we stuck out our arms and pretended to be birds.

A good Quihwa child memorized a hundred stories: trees who spoke, ravens who played tricks, men who chased whales in slender boats that skimmed the water like pelicans. My sister Lizzie and I learned these stories without writing them down, and the story of our mom and the whale became part of that lore. But in the summer of 1942, the world swelled so large we needed the newspaper to keep track of it all. There were German words, hard on our tongues. There were the names of islands in the south Pacific, whose syllables jumped around and made us laugh. So many stories, I persuaded my mom to run the generator so I could listen to the radio while she braided my hair. Gasoline was rationed, and my mom made it clear I was asking a lot. She said it would be cheaper to burn the perfume she kept in the square bottle on her dresser, but I reminded her that my dad had broken that bottle during a fight. I had heard it hit the wall. Ever since, the house had smelled like roses.

Lizzie's boyfriend, Billy, kept a siphon beneath the seat of his truck. The three of us used to drive around, and because I was small enough to crawl under a city-slicker's car, I learned the taste of petrol. I learned to accept dirt on the hem of my skirt. We salvaged scrap metal, too. After a storm, Lizzie, Billy, and I used to run down to the beach to pry cleats off the Weyerhaeuser log booms, the nails thick as fingerbones. Rusty cables lay twisted around themselves; we sold them to a junkman who came over from Port Angeles, and we always got a good price. Still, when I wanted a new dress pattern from the Sears catalog, my mom laid the cut-out against two lengths of red cloth—two, not one—and my sister and I got the same dress, mine loose, hers tight, her body showing some curves. Lizzie was pleased. She had already spent a dollar on a mail-order kit to set her straight black hair in a permanent wave. She was trying to hold Billy's gaze which, if you'd ever seen his sweet brown eyes, was not so easy. She permed her hair in a tub out back, and she got a whipping for it. I kept my hair long and braided stiffly down my back.

Because of the war, the Weyerhaeuser Company wanted extra saws in the woods. They were hiring Quihwa men, and the pay was too good to pass up. I never did learn how this aided the war effort, but that's what the company said, and our men pulled in their boats and disappeared into the woods. In a few weeks, the forests looked like the battlefields in *Life* magazine. There was no salmon on your table anymore; every two or three days, the men brought home money for corned beef, hams that you opened with a key, sugar and coffee. It made the women fat. Some men brought liquor if they had a weakness for that, and smokes, and stories they wouldn't tell. Then, before the smell of your dad's laundry was familiar again, he was gone for another hitch. They left their guns—so we could protect ourselves from "the Japs," but we were poor Indians and we didn't fancy our village much of a prize. If the Japanese ever stormed the Olympic peninsula, we hoped they brought their rain slicks. Still, in the attic of every house was a heavy bell, tethered to a rope that dangled into the kitchen from a hole in the ceiling. Emergencies only. My sister and I were forbidden to touch it. The thing is, my mom would never touch it either.

My mom and I liked to walk down the road to the beach to watch for submarines. The tides were lower than anyone could recall, and we could walk out at least a mile and splash our feet in a million shallow pools. The mighty sea had become a small thing you searched for, like a silver dollar fallen from your pocket. The tidepools were clicking with black mussels, and I waded to my thighs in these pools, my dress knotted around my waist in a way my mom said was too finicky.

We were out so far, you couldn't see the houses of the village anymore, and you no longer heard the log trucks jake-braking as they barreled out of the hills. It did not occur to me that my mom went on the beach to get away. She waded in after me, and I leaned against her chest, her great bear arms around me, her back to the world. She said my name, "Sylvie, Sylvie," again and again.

At night we would start up the generator, pull down the blackout curtains, and listen to the radio stations out of Seattle. I remember the battle of Midway; four Japanese carriers were sunk, and you already sensed the war had turned. Lizzie and I huddled around that radio, our mom's arms pulling us close. It reminded me of a time when my sister and I were younger and we sat in our mom's lap and listened to crazy stories about her relations; she was half Seminole, half white, and she had fled here with her mom at age ten because, her mom had said, the Olympics were as far from Florida as you could get and still be by the sea. Well, the three of us listened to the radio dramas after the news, and it was like Mom's old story time all over again, only instead of Uncle Jack fighting an alligator it was Phillip Marlow fighting crime. When you were twelve years old, and love meant feeling safe from everything in the world that could harm you, those times in your mom's lap were as good as it could ever be.

Around July Fourth, the men came home flush with cash, and we had a potlatch on the beach to celebrate the good times. My dad brought a company pickup with a dual axle, and we took it onto the sand. After a few beers, he bet he could drive that truck all the way out to the tidewater. My sister and I piled into the back. My mom rode in the cab. The tide was so low, driving into the tidal pools was like driving into a canyon. We drove over mussel beds that crunched under the wheels. We saw coral formations that should never have seen the sun or breathed the air. Well, of course the truck got stuck—the rocks were slick, you know—and the wheels slipped into separate pools and crowned the axle. Nothing was going to get that truck loose, and Lizzie and I had to run back for help. The bells in the village rang. When people made it out to the truck, my dad was at the wheel, and my mom was up to her thighs in the water, pushing against the tailgate. "You lifted a goddamned whale," my dad cried. She did lift that truck a little. She got the bumper onto her hip, and she was turning the truck around, but the waves were already coming in, and I saw the pain as she slipped, then tumbled, those waves rolling over her mighty shoulders, slow and smooth and slick. My dad stayed in the truck, sulking I guess, until the waves rose to the door handle and the truck began to take water into its bed. My mom, drenched and shivering, led us home. My sister ran off to a girlfriend's house for the night; that's where she said she was going, anyway. I remember thinking if the sea could swallow an entire truck, if the sea kept this kind of secret, it kept a thousand more.

Pride had a way of working itself into shame. That night, my mom lay in bed and gazed at the wall. As we waited for my dad to come home, I rubbed menthol and grease on my mom's back. She rolled cigarettes, the tiniest most delicate things, and sucked them down to embers that trickled off the edge of the bed. By midnight, I heard the fight through the wall. By one AM, it was my dad's voice cooing and promising in the old tongue never to do it again. By three AM, when my mom climbed onto the mattress I normally shared with Lizzie, she knew better than to tell me stories, because stories were supposed to tell the truth of the world, and only one truth needed to be told. I had heard enough. My mom didn't have to say anything.

He was gone by morning, and with the silence in the house we breathed again. Lizzie was back. She was sitting by the radio, trying to suck down a smoke and maintain a pose like Greta Garbo. Must have got the smokes from Billy. I sat on my bed, and my mom braided my hair, maybe an excuse to turn me away from her bruised face. I loved those strong fingers pulling on my scalp. It was a Quihwa custom: braiding gave me a sense of who I was, but it easily came undone. I liked it tight, and it took awhile. Of course, my mom let me listen to the radio. Something to fill the silence so we didn't have to come up with words.

I am old now, and I have seen that there are many ways for a woman to be strong, but growing up in that house beside the raging ocean, those ways were never taught to me. Instead I learned about shame. My mom should have fought back, or she should have told me why she didn't fight at all. And 1942 was a bad year not to feel strong. There was the war. There was this, too: I would soon find blood on the back of my skirt. And this: by July, the logs were deeper in the woods, like skittish salmon in the dark pools of a stream. My dad was gone for two weeks a hitch, and when he came home there was a hard, dense, solid sound to his fists. My sister would sneak out to be with Billy, while my mom kept me safe from my dad simply by getting in his way. If I dropped a jar of jam, my mom would hide me behind her back and take the whipping. Here is what I want to say: 1942 was a bad year because my mom decided to die. She would lie in bed, her battered face away from me. I would climb the mountain of her back and try to kiss her face, but she raised her hands. I caught glimpses of her eyes, swollen shut. I tried to crawl into her arms, that warm safe place, and listen to her stories, but she pushed me out of bed, my unbraided hair all loose and long. That is how I walked into the sun each day. When the sky was gray, I walked into a soggy rain. Either way, people knew: without those braids, I walked into the world ashamed.

Her dying became clear to me one morning late in July when we heard the bells again. This early in the morning, it had to be a whale. My mom yelled at Lizzie to put down her goddamn lipstick, take me to the beach, and see what the racket was. The tide would be out, so take a knife and a pail for mussels, and stay away from that goddamn Billy.

As we walked down the road, Lizzie shoved her pail into my hands, smoothed her dress, and shook loose her hair. When I reached the sand, Lizzie was not beside me anymore. She was heading toward a pickup. Billy. I yelled Lizzie's name. She glared and brought her fingertip to her lips, hush, then inclined her fist toward me. She knew I wouldn't tell. One time I did tell: they were kissing on the beach, and they climbed into the bed of the pickup and threw things out while I played in the sand. I could hear them laughing in there, then quiet for a long time, and when I told that quiet part to my mom, Lizzie got a whipping. Next day, Lizzie hit me in the back so hard that I fell and cut my face. She made me lie about how I fell on a rock. It was a betrayal. I didn't know what they were doing in the truck. I didn't know I'd done anything wrong.

Billy was eighteen, and he drove his dad's pickup everywhere. He didn't have permission, and maybe his dad knew, but his dad was up in the woods with the other men, and I do believe he would have whipped Billy for using all his gas if he had known. Billy drove Lizzie and me up to Port Angeles, and he made me suck gasoline from cars. He was a strong boy, and he should have been out there felling trees, but Lizzie was a real catch and he didn't want to lose her. Well, maybe he was strong, but my mom could take him, and he knew it. He never came closer than the end of the road. People said he was afraid of things.

My sister ran to Billy, who leaned against the side of the truck the way he must have seen Clark Gable do in a movie. Lizzie rested her hand on her hip when she stood next to him. I walked onto the sand with two pails.

The tide was way out again, leaking from one pool to the next. I wandered until the slope of the beach dropped away, until I felt like I was standing in the belly of the sea. Farther out, I saw a crowd of people at the water's edge, and I headed for them. It took five minutes for the dots to become the fat shapes of women who lived along the road.

"We found another whale . . ."

"Sylvie, where's your mom . . ."

"That's a lovely dress . . ."

"What are you gonna do with them pails, dig a sandcastle?" Maribel was two years older than me, and she could punch hard.

I pushed through the crowd and looked. There was the whale, stuck in a large pool, its gleaming back just showing above the water.

"Sylvie, go get your mom."

I stood and watched. The sun was bright on the whale's back. I thought of the Japanese floats we often found washed up on the shore. My sister and I saved them, the most beautiful things, gleaming balls of light and air and magic. Hold one up to the sun, stare through it without pain.

We tried to roll the whale, but it was like trying to loosen a box-car. The whale sighed and settled deeper into the sandy bottom. The sun was on our backs, and the skin of the whale was hot and steaming. As we stood in water up to our waists and heaved as one, we sang good old songs. We made a mighty voice like a man's, but the whale just rocked against our hips: I remember my hands pushing with all the other children's hands, as when you are pressing a rock, the side of a mountain, a solid thing. The women ceased rocking the whale, just stood along its side, shoulder to shoulder, those squat legs, wet cotton dresses, braids hanging limp and tired down their backs. These were strong hands; they cut wood and wrung water from clothes. But they were not men's hands, hard hands that could summon anger when it was needed most. Except Billy in that pickup, arching spray across the sand, all the men were gone.

Boys and girls smaller than me beat on the whale with sticks from the beach. A boy ran along the whale's back and slid down.

The big girl named Maribel shoved me, and I fell into the pool. "Your mama's not coming! You—"

I didn't hear what she said after that. I felt the cold, tasted the salt, then my skin brushed the smooth side of the whale. As I became used to the thick underwater noise, I heard my heartbeat strong and sure. I had often heard that sound at home, at night, when I was afraid. Then I heard a heartbeat beyond my own. The heart inside the whale. I pressed my ear to the whale's flank and listened. When I came up for air, my hair was wet and stuck to my back.

Everyone looked at me. The tide was around their hips, the surf creeping closer. Farther up the beach, gulls picked apart crabs. Billy had parked his pickup on the sand. He and Lizzie were in there, but you couldn't see them.

I said, "What about Billy?"

"Billie's a wimp."

"He has a pickup."

"That pretty boy's truck can't pull nothing. Besides, I seen Sylvie's mom lift the back of a truck. I mean I ain't seen it, but I heard about it."

My mother lay in bed hiding her black eyes, angry at the evil of the world.

* * *

When I was nine, I had a fight with my dad. We were all seated for dinner, and I announced that we weren't real Indians, on account of my mom being only half, and my dad, well, he had no relations, which, if you are Quihwa, is pretty much everything. Maribel had teased me, see. She had told me my braids didn't mean anything. Well, my dad slammed down his fork and came around the table, but I was faster, and I ran out the door and down to the beach. I ran into surf too strong, and I was carried out by the waves of a thick ocean. The water like sure arms bore me away, and then it was my mom's arms around me, lifting me back. She held me above her head with just one hand and waded back to shore. Above the roar of the sea, her booming voice: she told me about the Spanish influenza of 1918, of fishing accidents, alcohol, boarding schools, tribes with only three or four sad old women left and no one to share their stories, she told me names you respected best with silence, she told me everything else that made being an Indian so rare and fine. When we reached the house, that was when I saw my dad at the cistern, punching the ice away.

* * *

We lifted and heaved and rocked the whale back and forth. We sang songs until the rocking became a new song, but a rising tide was rolling in, smooth water spilling into the pool. Children couldn't touch the bottom, and they waved their arms and kicked their legs.

I twisted the water from my hair.

"Get your goddamned mom."

"She can't come. She fell. Hurt herself real bad."

"She been falling a lot lately. Always seems to land on her face."

We didn't sing anymore. We listened to the whale's breathing, slow as gusts of wind that spend themselves and leave silence in the air. The sun across the sky. My hands, all our hands, lay on the skin, the smooth skin, no barnacles, the clean patches of warm black. We stood in water up to our chests and looked at each other, none of us beautiful except my sister, a silhouette far up the beach, leaning against the pickup and fluffing loose her wavy hair.

One of the women put her arms around me, but I wanted my mom, and I began to cry. I shook her loose. I was the first to cry, but soon there were others. Did I tell you that my mother, when she held me, smelled like green leaves, she smelled like wood and tasted like salt? I swore if I had a child, I would hold her that way, let my child rub her mouth on my arm, her warm breath on my skin.

The water rose to our necks. The bigger waves rolled in and lifted you. They pushed the whale around too hard. When the tide rose with a surge, the whale lifted and thrashed, and we swam to get out of the way. The waves shook and roared. People trudged out of the water and back towards home. The thrashing whale settled down. It would never get out of the pool on its own.

"Sometimes they wash on the beach to die."

I wandered up the sand apart from everyone else, wet in my dress. Soon there was only sea and a warm wind that pelted my face with prickly sand. My hair was dry and loose as grass. I told myself my mom would braid it back, slick it with wax and braid it back tight and shiny and heavy on my spine, but in truth she hadn't done that for a long time.

Maribel jumped me on the road home. From behind a cedar tree she stepped out and dragged me back. "You go tell your mama she was too late." She slapped me. "And you won't tell on me, you won't tell a word, because everyone knows why your mama didn't come. What are you gonna do? You can't do anything." She pulled back my arms, yanked back my hair, and stuffed sand in my mouth. I turned my head and managed to bite her arm. Then she let me go. "You run, Sylvie, you run! You go tell your fat mama she was too late."

I did run. I ran up the road to my mom because a dozen times she had bent her back to the sea to save me. She had covered me up and taken the blows. She took on the waves of the sea, she held me and made me cough up salt water, breathed her air into my mouth.

My mom lay in the bed, buried under blankets, heaving slowly, sleeping in the mid-day dark of the blackout shades.

I said "Maribel beat me up."

She said "Get away from me."

"But Mom!"

"You want help, run away. You can't fight and win against such hands. I got cousins in Florida, and that's where you go. Take Lizzie, and you both run!"

I cried and cried. My mom could not read or write, but she made me memorize the names of her Seminole cousins. As I recited the order of highways and good places to sleep the night, restaurants where an Indian could beg for food, I persuaded myself this was only a game to fill the emptiness my mom never would. I would never go to Florida. We started the generator and listened to the radio. We listened to the news of the war, the crime serials, the music of the big bands. Always something to fill the space. We ate canned ham. I climbed into bed, lay against her, and did I tell her the story of everything she had missed today in her shame? No, I told my big strong mom how I loved her, and I braided her hair. I wrapped my skinny arms around her, sang the good songs from the radio where the words are chosen for you. I would someday find the words, as I am finding them now, far enough away, but not that day, not yet, I decided, and I congratulated myself on being twelve years wise.

"Where's Lizzie?"

"Out with Billy, I'd guess."

"What were the bells for, anyway?"

"Mama, do you remember that time I fell in and you pulled me back by my braid . . ."

That's where the story might end. I awoke in my own bed, beside my sister Lizzie, close enough to smell Billy's smokes in her hair. She was still wearing her red dress. Lizzie was the prettiest girl I had ever seen. If I had known she would be the only warm touch I would feel for many years, I would have put my arm around her sleeping skin and guarded her from anyone who would take her from me. Time was doing that on its own, I guess. The radio was on, telling news of battles far away. My mom was snoring; you could hear it through the wall. I stroked my sister's wavy hair.

The story could have ended there, simply because my mom was not a vengeful person. She always believed she was strong enough to take any pain. But shame is a weak thing, and vengeance is a weak thing too, and maybe they belong together. From up and down the beach, I heard bells ring, and I knew my mom had done something. I left Lizzie sleeping off another Billy night, and I slipped out the door, pausing only to notice that the rope which hung from our bell had been cut and allowed to fall to the kitchen floor.

On the beach, the women and elders and children of the village were standing around. They found the whale gone. Well, not gone. Rib bones were piled neatly as cordwood. The blubber was cut into strips and stacked. Buckets held ambergris. A hundred seagulls picked over the entrails, piled off to the side. It was the work of ten men.

We were left to imagine. My mom must have poured water over the whale's dying. She said the right prayers. The kick of the shotgun must have punched at her shoulder and the blast must have shaken her eardrums. Even at night, she must have seen the warmth leave the whale's body, and she could tell in other ways, the shape settling, cooling, no more warmth against its sides when she pressed her cheek to it. She knew what to do. She cut it up, said those prayers and cut it up and sang loud, not to drown out the bad feelings, but to feel strength in the chest, the pride that made you sing louder, bolder, Hear me, I have done something fine! She made short work of it, the blubber, the scrim, left just a little blood on the sand. My mom was so strong, she lifted the rib bones over her shoulder and carried them two at a time.

It took the whole village to start fires and roll out the rusty vats to cook the blubber down. Smelly nasty work, oil separating from flesh. The smudgy smoke turned your skin gray. There was no dignity to it, but none was deserved. The women poured ambergris into little jars and stored them away, to be passed around like honey at Christmas. They could light their homes and watch the shame illuminated on their faces.

Lizzie and Billy came down and began loading the jawbones into the pickup. These would bring a good price. I said, "Mom's sending us to Florida," and I recited the details of our trip as they were told to me. Lizzie sweetened on the idea when I took Billy's hand, stood real close to him, and smiled up at his face the way I had seen her do a hundred times. "Billy's gonna take us."

Billy frowned.

I opened the truck door, reached under the seat, and pulled out the siphon. Billy smiled. Oh, he had pretty eyes when he smiled.

* * *

We were Seminole Indians for eight weeks. Long enough for Billy to get Lizzie into trouble. I never did meet an uncle strong enough to fight an alligator, but you know what happens to a story over time. In the mornings, while Billy and Lizzie slept in the truck, I would unwrap my arms from myself and walk down to that silky Florida water. The surf barely covered my toes, but it was warm and blue while the Pacific was cold and clear, and I felt myself called deeper into something I did not understand. I pulled up the hem of my skirt and sloshed past my knees in the lapping waves.

When we came home to Washington, my mom and dad were buried in cedar boxes. It was impossible to know how it happened. Who pointed the gun at whom. Maybe my mom shot him, then shot herself, another bloody mess for someone else to clean up. Or maybe it was the other way around. It didn't matter. It was not the sort of thing anyone with dignity delved into. I have said too much, even now.

Billy shipped off to the south Pacific, and we never did learn what happened to him. Lizzie lost the baby. After the war, there was a ton of money kicking around, and they built a new high school in Port Angeles. In classrooms more crowded than our entire village, I learned what it meant "to pass," and I wore my hair in a ponytail like a good bobby-soxer. A little white in your skin hid a lot of secrets. I worked in the school library, shelving other people's stories, and I carried the books against my chest so the boys wouldn't look at me. My body grew up, but not my heart.

I can tell this story now because everyone I have mentioned is gone. My little band of Quihwa does not exist, the bloodlines having run too thin for the government's liking. There is no way you can verify any of my story. In 1942 there was a greater war for the world to fight, and what was left on our beach has long ago rinsed away. But I do wish to be believed. I hear it a lot: "You don't look like an Indian." Well, I have a secret, a way of braiding my still-black hair, which I can undo and hide any time. I can also put the braid together again strong and shiny, tight enough to pull on my eyebrows.

You have to understand the secrecy of my story. We were people who kept words to ourselves like stones in our pockets. We spoke a language only books understand anymore. And we were just women, the keepers of private stories—the men's voices were in the trees, silenced by saws. But there was also this: on that July day, I don't mind saying now, I was ashamed: a whale lay gasping on the beach as my mother lay hiding in a blanket ashamed of her eyes. She could have left any time. She knew it. She couldn't say it, but I am saying it now. I spit the sand from my mouth. This is my way to be strong.

Joseph Radke

CHANCES OF PRECIPITATION

They never knew—or knew for the first time,
The [word missing] *of the rain*
         from *The Last & Lost Poems* by Delmore Schwartz

The woman in the doorframe
with one hand in the top corner,
hip cocked into the groove of the strike plate,
is neither the door opened nor
the door closed, neither barred nor unlocked.

Just as the crack of too bright sunlight
through the blinds is not your soul and
the heat rising off you in the humid morning
is not your spirit ascending.

This is how the highway feels:
that mirage of wetness an illusion
without symbol. When it does come,

the word missing in the rain
brings its own relief.

Catherine Sherman

THREE-TOED SLOTH

Under the rain forest,
      light punctured, the sky no more
than a drape cloth over
      the imperturbable sun,
you and your baby hang,
      a pair of wool serapes,
vacuum bag and duster.
      The silver ribcage of the
tree canopy grows to
      encapsulate you. Each branch
is an arm extended.

You and your baby choose
      isolation, your spirit's
mind quiet, still as roots.
      You know where not to go, not
where perambulation
      is a matter of dragging
your burlap sack body
      like a paralytic. Sloth,
you are no imbecile.
      You do not call attention
to yourself in the still-
      ness of the dark, blade-shaped leaves.

Your elimination
      habits are worth example;
weekly defecations
      made at the base of the tree.

Your fur is a pond of
    color, sometimes emerald,
where moths delicate as
    ash or snow emerge, take flight.

Allan Peterson

Air Above The Valley

How many do you miss? Name them
starting with lost dogs.
At any moment there are more
than you expected,
more than the marble reliquary steps
of December and January
leading to their names, and the worlds
that travel with this one
are re-peopled like phone books.
These are the fine points of all that matters:
carbonate questions,
how many hawks it takes to rewind
the air above the valley, the loaded oceans,
how many patterns came to my fingers as I dried,
like veins to cicadas,
like wasps known by their wing compartments.
I am about to turn the page.
The oak reading over my shoulder puts a leaf in
to save its place.

Allan Peterson

CURE

Initially his anger was a thing like a plowed field
where nothing was planted. One could see the land

opened against its will, the coulter a knife at its throat.
Sometimes over a long winter he would re-read books

from the back to make them seem new again,
dream the drowned boy back bursting to the surface

of the mill pond for a gasp of breath and the broom
of light sweeping itself backwards out the door he kicked closed.

It was finally the light like so many stories of creation.
The light that made it little by little a day later
and the loons telling him nightly they were lonelier by far.

INTERVIEW: SANDRA KOHLER

 Sandra Kohler's second collection of poems
The Ceremonies of Longing (Pitt Poetry Series,
2003) was winner of the 2002 AWP Award
Series in Poetry. Her poems have appeared
recently in *Diner*, *The Colorado Review*, *The
New Republic*, and *Prairie Schooner*. She has
recently moved from Selinsgrove, Pennsylvania, a small town on the Susquehanna River,
to Boston. She misses the herons.

*What bit of advice do you wish someone had told you when you first began
your vocation as a writer?*

What makes you a writer is writing. You don't need to define yourself
as gifted or even talented or extraordinary, you just have to work at
your craft. That means writing regularly. And when you do that, you
are entitled to the pleasure it will give you: the almost transcendent
pleasure of losing yourself in the work, of "flow": being so totally
absorbed by something that uses you fully that you surface from
writing a poem feeling as if you've just run five miles.

In my version of the world Virginia Woolf's novels would be more
widely read than the *Da Vinci Code*, *Volver* would win Best Picture at
the Academy Awards and Mahler's *Fifth Symphony* would play at least
once a day from every radio in the world.

Can you tell something about the origin of your poems, how they were written, where, what might have influenced them?

Ah, can I ever. Think of the Susquehanna River, mornings. I used to be a runner. In my late fifties, no longer allowed to jog after a hip replacement, I slowed to walking. Almost every morning I walked along the Susquehanna River in Selinsgrove, Pennsylvania, where I lived. I'd loved the river, running; but walking permitted me to see it, begin to know it. The first winter after the hip operation I noticed the occasional great blue heron along the banks; each time I saw one, I felt my heart lift up (yes, I'm stealing from Wordsworth). Because I gradually observed that there were certain places where I saw one, I began to think that he, like me and the other walkers along the river, were "regulars," that I was seeing the same heron over and over. And when I thought about naming him, what came (bad pun) was Heraclitus. Which of course for a writer obsessed with change led interesting places. I found myself writing about the herons in my daily morning writing and on the small pad I always carried with me as I walked. Eventually the idea of a series of Heraclitus poems took shape; the poems published here are most of them.

Which desire can you not detach from (a question mostly for—but not only—Buddhists)?

I love this question. I'm not formally a Buddhist, but think of myself as something of an accidental Buddhist. To a close friend who is one, and who sees Buddhist elements in my work, I've said that I can't be one because attachment is what I'm all about as a poet. Attachment to a few deeply loved people, to my own mortal body's life, to the earth and its transient beauty. Recently I've been struggling with this issue because I moved, just six months ago, from a house with a garden that I'd spent ten years creating. I am trying to practice detachment from that garden: not mourn it, not want to find out about whether it's being preserved and cared for. And from the river and the herons and my morning walks in Selinsgrove. Hard as this is, it's comparatively easy when I think of my husband, my son, my desire to keep living.

What must you do before you can sit down to write?

Almost every single morning I get up, make a cup of coffee, get out my lap desk, narrow-lined yellow 8x11" pad and Pilot Precise Rolling Ball pen (black, extra fine), sit down in a rocking chair in my living room, and start doing my "morning writing"—free writing for half an hour or so. This has become a deeply sustaining ritual for me. It's not the only time I write, of course; most days I follow this with exercise and breakfast and then sit down at my desk, computer, where I work on making poems. But my "morning writing" produces the raw material from which I eventually make almost all my poems, and it maintains my connection to the springs of my own creativity. As to sitting down to work later in the day, I try not to have anything that I have to do before getting started: it seems vital to me to have writing be my first priority. Of course there are times when reality interferes but a habit of having the writing come first makes it easier to get back at it when the emergency is over or the chaos has subsided.

What is your most significant source of frustration as a writer? What do you love most about the act of writing?

The difficulty of getting published, especially book publication. I'm not interested in posthumous fame—I'd like readers and recognition while I'm alive to enjoy them, though I also want my poems to be read two hundred years from now. What I love most about the act of writing is the loss of self, the suspension of time, the absorption that comes when you are fully engaged. You are not your ego, you are not you, you are totally immersed in process, in the work of the moment, in a suspended now that is liberating and exhilarating even though one is not at the moment conscious of being either liberated or exhilarated.

When did you first begin to identify yourself as a writer?

Probably by the age of eleven. I remember walking down the block I lived on one night when I was that age, composing my first "real" poem, about unrequited love, in my head. I thought it was for the boy in my junior high class I had a crush on; later, I realized it was a poem to my father who was about to marry my stepmother.

Sandra Kohler

Heraclitus and Others

—"Character," said Heraclitus at the beginning of Western thought, "is fate."

Yesterday's upheavals, emailed rebuke from
my son, phone calls from my sister, brother.
Distance and closeness; the mystery of other
people, of each of us. I dream of an arena,
a hospital, a prison: great dark buildings. Labor
and delays, dinners and healing. There is wind
pushing the skinny twigs that top the mulberry,
a branching fragile as reeds. The hills across
the river are lost, the world ends at the creek.
I'm going to go out and walk in the cold, in
foglight. Look for the heron, find the interrogative
curve he makes in the scratched geometry of
reeds, watch as he snakes forward, step by step,
Hindu dancer, his neck leading, retreating, slow
progression, each step testing the new river anew.
Yesterday heron after heron, six sightings—all
of them flew when seen, sensing when I stop, stare.
The thunderous cloud mesa is turning rose streaked
now. Will my poems in twenty years be single words:
rose/thunder/heron? I decide that the biggest heron
I see, the old one, is Heraclitus. The rest are his sons,
daughters, grandchildren perhaps. Now all the clouds
are fire-ridden, bright auroral signals of some joy
I don't understand. My sister will fly to France
and remain unchanged, my brother will refuse to
give up one sip of his cup of bitterness, my son
will build a future using love and anger at loving

angry parents for blocks, mortar. I will dream of
a hundred journeys, a hundred destinations, a
hundred changes and take one new step a decade,
though the heron announces we are new each
morning. A Heraclitan fire burns through all
our days whether or not we raise our eyes
to the sky where it flames in mysterious
hieroglyphs that encrypt our nature,
our characters, our fates.

Sandra Kohler

Heraclitus, First Sighting

A small bar of cloud over the hill is radiant with
arrival. I'm suspended here, riding like the clouds,
a casual flotilla drifting south. On the horizon
the sky's pale apricot, green, gold: the colors of
fruit just beginning to ripen. For years I've watched
my child ripen: a child no longer, he is hard and
firm, tree not fruit, process not product. A great
swooping line in the clouds, upside down arc of
a mountain, just over the hills, mirroring them.
Above, the sky's blue, halcyon. I could garden this
afternoon. I could sleep all morning. My dreams
are just out of reach. There was a moment, waking,
when I remembered them, a moment when I forgot.
Forgetting is the house you live in, the familiar body
you turn to, the warm place in the bed where you
want to sleep, leaving a cold stretch of it empty.
Yesterday, walking, I saw a heron at the bottom
of Pine Street, where there's a slope to the river
and ducks congregate: one heron, weird graceful-
awkward arc, standing in the nacreous light, a pale
silhouette, cumbrously still. I stood there, watched,
then, moving toward him on grass, the footsteps
I couldn't hear spooked him; slowly, awkwardly,
he took flight, spreading vast wings, skimming
the surface of the river. The sky was a blessing,
strewn, arrows of cloud going off in all directions,
reflections on the white mirror of the cold river.

Sandra Kohler

Heraclitus' Food

A November sky: layered, obscure. It's dry,
muted, wind-tossed. In my dream I'm
bleaching a sheet, unable to get out the stain
my purple sash left on it. What taint can't I
cleanse? Past failures, mistakes, omissions
bleed onto the surface of an intimate refuge,
in the hues of the kimono I put on to take off
for love. At five AM the phone rings twice.
Dread. I lie awake wondering what disaster
or malign intent it signals. The wind's higher,
turbulent, I want to go back to bed. Last night
I stayed up into the morning, wanting time out
of time, uncounted, unaccountable. I'll walk,
I'll check the rain gauge, I'll count herons. I'll
open my eyes to the brilliant green flame of
the grass, the dulled amber fire of the leaves,
the face the river presents, clarity or mottled
dark. After a day without walking or herons
I'm restless, displaced: my skin doesn't fit,
my body's an exile. Walking yesterday, I see
Heraclitus on the fallen tree at the boat slip,
struggling with the big fish in his beak. It falls
back into the shallows, he digs avidly, pulls it
out of the mud. The world feeds us, starves us,
sates us. Last winter one of the herons choked
to death on a fish. What determines whether
we find food, use it, choke on what could be
sustenance? Wrestling with what's large,
obstinate, bitter, we fail to see sweet fish
in the shallows that would nurture us,
starve in the midst of plenty.

Sandra Kohler

Heraclitus and the Heart Transplant

My sister's husband, an only child, envied the bond
he imagined she and I had. On the anniversary of
his death, I wake just before dawn from dreaming
I'm to have a heart transplant. It will improve my
life, but recovery will take months, years—who
knows when I will be able to do what I can now?

These days I mourn the sister I don't have and
never did, but believed in. I need a change of heart.
Yesterday, at the river, I walk past the boat launch,
not thinking about how far I'm going, absorbed in
how the river, the hills, the sky, the sky, the hills in
the river all seem held in a dulled silver mirror

which dims, perfects them. A great blue heron rises
near the shore, its wings wide, wild, gives its harsh
awkward cry, circles the river. I haven't seen one since
before my surgery. I've forgotten my body, able to
walk as long as I care to, feeling as free from limit
as I did when I could run every day, in any weather.

I could grieve at not being allowed to run any more;
I have chosen not to. I choose morning and mist,
the birds gathering, blue jay and cardinals eating
berries in the pink dogwood, dull sparrows gleaning
the lawn. At the river, Heraclitus is ready to migrate,
knowing winter is coming, knowing how to change.

Sandra Kohler

What Heraclitus Said

Above the horizon, as if outlining the hill's
crest, a blaze of white on slate blue, not break
but scar, gap, lacuna. Strange, untoward. Lights
stream along the bypass, delicate, gold, festive
stars in the blue gray light. Light and the snow
and days of a private joy, private grief. Yesterday
I owned my body, today nothing is mine but
its scars. There are rivers invisible as the dust we
breathe, there is air flowing into our lungs from
a century's buried wars. When morning gets up
and dresses and goes for a walk, it will not find
me. If Heraclitus is hunched at the river's edge,
claws scoring the ice, I won't be there to see him.
Lacunae, gaps: in dreams, in the roads you are
walking, stairways you climb, broken stones,
the sudden treachery of earth, the grave unfolding
of your life. Winter is silent enemy: what I see
and what I fear marrying what I can't see, don't
fear. What Heraclitus said, I read, is that the world
is a bow, a lyre: tense, balanced; weapon, instrument.
Will it make war or music today, hunt me or
serenade? The lyre sings to the bow, a Heraclitan
anthem: hunt and fish, track and gather: you can
not exhaust the flesh and fowl of reality, the hidden
bounty of day's ambiguous manna and mana.

Sandra Kohler

HERON AND QUESTION

Fog again, the morning soaked in it.
In the garden, patches of cobwebs in low
clumps of flowers, nests of caught mist.
I need to walk, I need to remember my
dreams, I need . . . This is not the time
for lists. Birds strung on telephone wires
fly off as if falling, plunging straight
into blankness. This is a time and place
for anything. Anything goes. *Gone* was
my son's first verb. I feel blank, plunging.
I talk to my sister and she is brittle, cheery,
shut. I am becoming cold, judgmental.
I will those who have married disaster
to rear the children of that union, owning
consequence. I forget all the ways I've walked
away from my acts over the years. Where is
the beginning and end of this fog? What is
its center, its heart of whiteness? Dreaming
of unanchored branches that clutch at stony
rubble, leaf out, alive, from concrete, stone,
macadam, no soil at the roots, I imagine my
family ignores me, my brothers worry only
about my sister's woes, I am left to make
my own way. Jealousy's face is a sister's,
the face of indifference a brother's: both
reflect my own. What we know and what
we don't know each wounds. At the river,
the heron gives a cry strange and awkward
as its stance, its elegant neck curved into
a question like the white wisps that rise
from the satin surface of the waters.

Sandra Kohler

Heron, Present and Absent

Things keep their secrets.
—Fragment 10, *The Fragments of Heraclitus*

i.

There you are
in your favorite spot
arched, hieratic,
posing, stretching
your cobra neck,
contracting,
lifting those
sticks of leg in
slow steps,
then quick jabs
of beak
plunge
into the river
hovering
over the
water's
gleam,
gleaner,
fisher,
suddenly
still
aware

ii.

Magic scrim, stream
floating veils of mist
sun's white disc:
shadows of
fishermen cast
lines for ghost fish
Heraclitus,
diplaced,
shifts downriver
huddles on a branch
at the water's edge
opens his beak
closes it again,
stolid
still

iii.

Yesterday, weedy growth
along the shore gone gold
walnuts cracking under
a car's wheel like gunfire
Heraclitus
at the end
of my walk posed
doubled
by water:
I want to bring
him back, prey,
precious ore,
miraculous fish
I caught to feed

my friend, son,
brother,
love.

How we're overcome
by the impulse
to share something
we love, shower it
on others, manna;
how often
the gift fails,
is not
received.

iv.

The river this morning
a gift, a grant of seeing.
Looking for won't do, only
looking. Yesterday the baby
geese in clusters of fur
on the wet grass, huddles
of pale gold fuzz.

The light is riven
given streaming as
fast as the current
white transformation
the flickering ever
changing flow
the shimmering
unending
source

the web of birdsound
squittering blackbirds
in the stubby tree
a weave of branches
stubble lace seed and pod
white boned sycamore
scrag of nut trees.
Is that the corpse
of Heraclitus?

v.

Mimosa's golden seeds
rustle like taffeta.
Where do you go,
Heraclitus,
when the spring melt
turns the river to flood
and plain, a spreading
road of water
and all the ducks
shelter in puddles
and leas of sedge,
edge, shore gone
marshland? On
the coldest days
you trod the ice.
Now your gift
is absence.

vi.

I would like to have
wings like the heron's
that reach, that breadth
of span, expanse.
We are so small and
frightened in the light.
We need to grow
ourselves out of our
fear, our pettiness.
I imagine a heron's
wings in my shoulders,
the muscles of my upper
arms, straining,
stretching,
spreading.

vii.

The herons I can't
summon by wish
won't come
by whim
it is their will
to be elsewhere
not here
my morning
is full of
their refusal.

viii.

The river without
herons: a diminished
thing, lifeless,
dispirited.
They are my wild
swans, my muse
of absence.
Praise absence.
Give back to
the river
what you took
from it
presence
spirit
breath
inspiriting

ix.

In my dream I'm swimming
in the river and herons
land—near me,
on me.
Those great swooping
wings I see spreading
and taking off:
in the dream, on
the river, they are
swooping down,
closing, a heron lands
on my arm, perches
there.

Anointing,
confirmation:
I am in and
of the river,
Heraclitus'
world.

x.

That a heron is back
at last year's chosen haunt,
the fallen tree jutting
out into the river
near the gravel slope
where boats put in
seems reassurance
sign of normalcy
regeneration
a heartless proof
of life going on
despite us

xi.

Is it the herons
that have returned
or my ability
to see them?

xii.

Is your return ironic
note—the longed-for
coming when it's no
longer comfort—or a
promise: recurrence,
order, healing, no
matter what?

There's no reading
the heron
perhaps there's no
heron but
reading

xiii.

Even what is
contained
and isolate in us
is drawn, curious,
to the face in that
mirror
the other
the passing stranger
to whom we blurt
passing some secret
of the self
like the heron
wild solitary
awkward drawn
despite himself
to the manmade

world along
the shore
battered boats
engines
weathered
piers

xiv.

Being a poet:
if the heron's there,
you write about it;
if not, you write
about its
absence.

xv.

We the obsessed
will always find
the objects of our
obsession find
or imagine
what difference
it is the light
in which we view
that shifts, changes
at dawn or dusk
the mind's
shade or gleam

Ah Heraclitus
interrogation
mark inscribed

on the mutable
waters curved
s of sign
signet
seal

An Ordinary Story

Millicent Meibert suffered from the inability to be ordinary. Her mother wouldn't tolerate an ordinary girl.

"Do something special," Mrs. Meibert would say. "You have an exceptional brain."

Millicent grew up with exceptional qualities, none of which she could name, and a dangerous feeling that she was to do something hugely important. Her first attempt was poetry: none of the lesser art forms would do. Millicent's mother swelled with pride. She told Millicent that there was no doubt that she had influenced her daughter's decision by always having books lying around, practicing *Reader's Digest* word games, and doing crossword puzzles. Millicent's special contribution to the world would undoubtedly be poetry. The young Ms. Meibert quit her advertising job in Los Angeles and moved to the South to study writing.

"I'm very pleased," Mrs. Meibert clucked and cooed to her daughter over the phone the first time Millicent called from her new writer's studio apartment. Millicent had seen a dead armadillo on the roadside earlier that morning, a metaphor for her old dead life, inevitably the subject of a riveting poem, and she felt her heart grow with excitement to begin her stupendous accomplishments.

But being a poet had a depressing effect on Millicent. She wore long skirts and long sweaters, long jackets, and long earrings to match her long hair. She found a long and depressing boyfriend who took her on long car trips to see places like Graceland. He held her hand through the long depressing month of August. She stayed for four long years.

When the poetry and the poet didn't work out, Millicent went home to Los Angeles where her mother lived and returned to her old job as an advertising executive, overseeing, but not dispensing, quips.

She wore suits, and her mother, depressed and dejected, tried to take her to plays. *Molière*. Mrs. Meibert rambled on about how Millicent had to go with her.

"You need intellectual stimulation," Mrs. Meibert said to her daughter one afternoon on the phone. Millicent knew that her mother thought advertising drab.

"I don't need intellectual stimulation. I have a job," Millicent said. "And call me Millie. It's a better name for business." She knew the shortened and *ordinary* version of her name would annoy her mother. But Millie didn't care. This was her life now. She bent a paperclip in two. She liked to untwist and rework them into miniature abstract sculptures and then throw them in the trash.

Her mother sighed into the phone. "You are still Millicent to me," she said.

Millie sighed back and wrinkled her nose. She wished her mother would just leave her alone so she could get some work done. Always work to be done, facts, figures, paperclips, things to stick sticky papers on so she could find them later and say, "Hmm. Now why did I stick that there?" or "Oh, I'm glad I didn't let this one get away from me." Then she would tuck the paper in the lower basket of her In Box and never look at it again. Phone calls. Calendars. The numbing space behind the words on the gray page of the computer screen. Millie was not going to a play by Molière. Not tonight. Tonight after work, she had her coupons.

Millie had lots of coupons. Mrs. Meibert constantly gave her coupons for tampons and cat food. When Millie was a poet, this was good. She needed them, but now that Millie had an executive job, the incoming coupons grew exponentially. She told her mother that she didn't use them, and her mother sent her more. Every Tuesday they arrived in the mail with newspaper clippings of play critiques, book reviews, book signings to attend, and lectures. Things were circled. Expiration dates and places and times.

In protest, Millie bought her tampons and cat food in the most outrageous places she could think of: gas stations and gourmet markets. She took pleasure in telling her mother that the Gas Queen

Station didn't accept coupons for Kitty Krunchies. Or she would ask her mother, "Do you ever see coupons for organic tampons? Only Mrs. Greedies Gourmet sells those."

Mrs. Meibert would glare and say, "I don't know what's becoming of you," and Millie would blink. She knew. Her life was taking a twist. She was becoming one of those people who never had groceries in her refrigerator, who purchased every meal, who stepped into an elevator every day and rode to the sixteenth floor, looked out her sooty window and dreamed of getting away from it all on some sunny, remote island beach, fruity drink in hand, tanned lover on her arm—just for a weekend. She worked hard when the fog cleared from her brain. At least once a week, she stayed late, always glancing around the corner of her office door expecting to see something fantastic, like a six-foot-four clown in pink pajamas who smiled and offered her a balloon—just something different to brighten her world. She wondered, where had her poetry gone? What happened to the hours spent strolling down the wide well-stocked aisles of Piggly Wiggly, searching for bargains on Friday afternoons? That's where coupons for tampons and cat food really mattered. How could she have metamorphosed overnight into a woman with suits, stacks of coupons she'd never use, and enormous cat food charges on her gas card? *Millie.* That's who she was now.

One afternoon in the cereal aisle of the grocery store, she met Albert. He'd asked her if she'd ever tried Cinnamon Clusters, and she had because she'd worked on the ad campaign: "They're Seriously Cinnamon." Albert liked that. He had a thing for cereal. He was a connoisseur.

On their first date, he proudly showed her his pantry full of unopened cereal boxes, mostly children's cereal, sweet with pink globs that bobbed in the milk. The first morning she stayed over, she wanted an egg. But Albert was so happy to open his cereal closet for her, let her pick whatever she wanted that Millie couldn't make an egg request. No. She put the cereal in her mouth with her fingers. Sweetness. Maybe she should give him some coupons.

Albert was an executive, too. Not a reluctant one like Millie, but a dedicated executive despite, he explained, his short-timer status.

Short-timer meant he was leaving his sales job at the paper supplies company soon. He didn't know where he was going, but he had decided he needed a break from executive life and had to quit. Millie decided it was a phase. Like her poetry phase and the aisles of Piggly Wiggly specials, the cricketed nights, her tiny brick apartment surrounded by trees hung heavy with vines and fermenting leaves, sips of wine at any time at all, and mornings where she sat on her thrift store couch in a patch of sunlight and wrote until noon. That was a phase. Advertising Executive. This was real life. Paying off bills.

Whatever would Albert do with his free time?

He planned to create stained glass. He would buy a blowtorch. He would make her sunny, colorful window hangings of hummingbirds and peonies. Maybe an owl. Millie pictured a huge stained glass rat. What if he made her a giant stained glass rodent with teeth and yellow eyes? Very nice. Yellow eyes that glowed in the sun.

Mrs. Meibert, who had been a fan of the poet boyfriend, did not want to meet Albert. "He sounds very fancy," she said when Millie told her about the dinner he had taken her to. There was a new restaurant at the L.A. Zoo, which had several good reviews from the most respectable culinary experts. The Zoo, Too was its name and getting in was almost impossible. Albert had swung it and Millie was thrilled to eat there. The long depressed poet had never taken her out. He'd preferred to dine-in on baked potatoes, broccoli, and black beans.

The Zoo, Too has an intimacy only close proximity to animals can afford, wrote one reviewer.

The waiter informed them that the primate tables were the most popular, and they had lucked out. There were bear, lion, and gazelle tables, as well as several other mammals. Millie was seated next to an orangutan, looking at her from behind the glass. The monkey made her feel a little shy, as if he were a hairy chaperone. Albert seemed a little embarrassed, too. He leaned the menu up against the window to block the orangutan's stare. Then he took her hand.

Mrs. Meibert thought fancy restaurants were anti-intellectual. And when Millie said, "But he's from Detroit," Mrs. Meibert said,

"Well, how do you know he's not a gangster?" Millie blinked. Her mother was getting more cantankerous every day. *Molière* was out. She was now going to salons.

Her mother called her at work one morning and invited her.

"Are you interested, Millicent," Mrs. Meibert cleared her throat, as if to indicate she was about to say something very significant, "in the Hormonal Variances of Mexican Pop Stars in the Early Twentieth Century?"

Millie peered at the phone receiver. Then she placed it back to her ear, mumbling, "I guess so," and read an email.

"Good. There's a salon this Thursday night at seven-thirty, and I'd like you to come. A brilliant young Ph.D. candidate is reading from her latest paper. It would be good for you to meet some of these smart women."

"I have a hair appointment." It was the only time Millie could get her hair done with her busy executive schedule and dates with Albert.

Mrs. Meibert sniffled. "Well, maybe some other time. Some other day, I guess."

The irony of the dueling salons hit Millie later that afternoon while she was at an executive meeting, doodling as all reluctant executives do. She drew a large pine tree, two stars, and "SALON. SALON" in thick blue ink. She thought about how in the past she had been inspired to write poems about the irony of such a situation. Even mundane experiences such as the meeting she was in might have carried a seed of inspiration, but she didn't have the heart to write now. Somehow her will had left her. She had an inkling of the cause of its disappearance. The poet, of course. He had made her feel so bad. He forced her to compare herself to a stray dog eating garbage out of a dumpster. Imagine. He hadn't said it, but it was still his fault. He made her say it. The poet had moved her to make the comparison, that was the problem, Millie thought.

They'd been sitting in his car in the parking lot of a bookstore. They had just been to his little sister's wedding in Jackson, and Millie, wondering when it would be their turn, had waited patiently through the ceremony, the dinner and dancing, aching to ask him *when?* He had avoided her all night. Her pouts and hypnotic stares from across the red Victorian room of the reception hall didn't make him turn on his worn down heel and propose to her. He mostly dodged her, left her sitting with his cousins, aunts, and several small children.

But he had to drive her home. He couldn't avoid her then, and once in the car, parked behind the old bookshop, she asked him if he ever thought they would get married. Instead of telling her "Maybe," or "Some day," or "We're too good for that," he told her that he hated her shoes. He hated all the shoes in her closet. While she stared at him, her eyes brimming, she learned he hated other things too. He hated her floral sheets and pillows. He hated the way she collected angels. He hated the angels on all her floral sheets and pillows, in her posters, and in the depths of her closet between her shoes. He hated almost everything she liked. Shopping. Restaurants. Hairdos. Her cat. He looked at her with disgust, and she realized, even though he had been her boyfriend for four years, he hated her too. Not just the little things about her but all of her.

"You'll never be a poet," he told her. "You have too much stuff."

Then across the dark parking lot, she noticed a thin, black dog, standing on a mound of garbage in a dark green dumpster. She had no idea how the mutt had climbed up there.

She told the poet she was that dog.

"I want that garbage," she said. "I'll snoot around until I get it."

She smiled. She still liked herself for saying that. She knew somehow it was a testimony to her tenacity, her ability to find something good in the mounds of crap life dispensed. But there was something embarrassing about it, too. She had, after all, compared herself to a most ordinary dog, pushing its nose through the rancid leftovers of other people's lives.

Now sitting in the drab, ill-lit conference room, half-heartedly listening to the big boss talk about improving client service, Millie wondered if she still had the will of that dog to get what she wanted. No, she thought, she'd lost her determination somewhere, maybe in Jackson. That garbage dog had dug it up, shown it to her, and eaten it right before her eyes, or perhaps, it had departed with the poet. He'd stolen it away when he'd left her standing in the parking lot crying goodbye. Now she put on her executive suit every day, stepped into the elevator, and tried not to forget what *caesura* meant, then realized that she already had.

After the meeting, she returned to her office and listened to several voice mails from her mother urging her to reconsider the salon.

"Every intellectual woman in Los Angeles will be there."

Millie sighed. Her mother was always inviting her to events where every intellectual woman in Los Angeles would be, and Millie knew the invitations would continue as would the post-salon reports, each one making her feel insufficient, less accomplished, more ordinary.

"There were, maybe, seventy-five women there all honoring Mrs. So-and-So for her fine contributions to such-and-such." Then, "There were 200 intellectual women there honoring Ms. Bla-bla for bla-de-bla. You really should have gone." The numbers of women would continue to grow with the lengthening of the days and the shortening of the year. "A thousand women, all intellectuals, all accomplished. You might have met someone to talk to."

Finally, "Five thousand women, throngs of them," she imagined her mother saying. "They had the most fascinating brains, the size of Volkswagen bugs, outstanding, intellectuals. You should have gone." But Millie would always be too busy. She couldn't bear to hear her mother introduce her as, "My daughter, the poet Millicent Meibert." She knew her face would turn red as she explained she'd never really published anything, but once upon a time, she'd tried really hard.

The rest of the day escaped her in a series of late meetings. Millie missed her hair cut because of a final really-late meeting and ended up going to the grocery store with Albert. He had found a two-for-one deal on the pink cereal with peanut-butter-flavored crunchies, and he had to buy them even though he had three unopened boxes of the same thing in his pantry.

"But why, Albert?" Millie asked, rubbing her fingers on the smooth cardboard edge of a box cradled in Albert's mammoth arms.

"I'm looking for a good deal," Albert said, winking.

Millie looked at wide-eyed Albert staring at the brightly colored cereal boxes, four now clutched to his chest. Millie wondered if she could be considered a good deal. Once maybe, but now she wasn't sure. She was too ordinary, cog-in-the-wheel material. That's all. Her guy seemed ordinary too, but she liked that. She liked that he liked cereal, grocery stores, and stained glass, all colorful things.

She stared at one of the red boxes full of the peanut butter and pink stuff. She tried to see it through Albert's eyes. What was the attraction? The cartoonish packaging offered fun, health, integrity, comfort, self-confidence. All those ordinary things. She sighed. They were so hard to get.

Then the tag line popped into her head. *Eat me, I'm fun*, the cereal seemed to say.

"Eat me, I'm fun," Millie mumbled.

Albert grinned and grabbed another.

In the parking lot, Millie and Albert ran into Mrs. Meibert. She had gone to the same store to buy gold fish crackers for the salon because it was just a block away. Intellectuals always ate gold fish crackers, Mrs. Meibert once told Millie. Mrs. Meibert didn't know why but she thought it might have something to do with fish being brain food. She knew the crackers didn't have fish in them, but there was something meaningful in the suggestive power of their shapes.

Although they'd never met before, Albert hugged Mrs. Meibert. Millie could tell from the way Mrs. Meibert smiled and nodded that this was a good thing for him to do. Then Mrs. Meibert suggested they all go to the salon. Millie's legs turned to wood. Albert said okay and that he just needed to put his cereal in the trunk. Mrs. Meibert clapped her hands and bustled off to her car. Millie thought about saying she was busy. Albert and her mother could go alone. They could be intellectual together.

While Albert carefully placed the bags in the trunk, Millie counted to ten. At least her mother seemed to like Albert. Maybe she should just get this over with.

"Albert," she whispered. "You don't know what it's like at these things. Promise you won't hate me in the morning."

"No sweat, Peaches," he said. Albert liked to call her Peaches. "What are you afraid of?"

"I'm afraid my mother will scare you off," she said and slammed the trunk. He laughed and she winked, but secretly, she worried that when Albert saw her next to those smart women, he, like the poet, might think she wasn't good enough.

The salon was located in the fellowship hall of a nearby church. Millie and Albert drove over then sat in his car in the dimly lit parking lot and waited for Millie's mother, who was a slow driver. Taking advantage of the few minutes that she had alone with Albert, Millie wanted to tell him how silly this lecture was going to be. She needed to prepare him for her humiliation, but she wasn't sure how to explain. She thought about saying something joking like, "These things always put me to sleep," or "Watch out for the head bob." She thought about telling him about her ex-boyfriend. Instead she said, "I don't know why you even like me, Albert."

He looked at her quizzically.

"What I mean is—you don't mind that I like my cat, wear floral pajamas, sleep on floral sheets, and have lots of shoes and will most likely buy more soon?" She braced herself for his answer.

"I like all that stuff," Albert said.

"But it's all so ordinary."

Albert moved in for a kiss.

"You're not bran flakes, Baby," he whispered. "You're a very special mix."

Behind him, Mrs. Meibert's face appeared at the window, reminding Millie briefly of the orangutan at *Zoo, Too*. Her mother tapped on the glass with her car keys.

"Hurry, hurry."

Albert kissed her swiftly and pulled away, rolling up his shirt-sleeves before getting out of the car.

Millie pushed her door open and paused. She wanted to compose herself, breathe in a bit of night air, chant if necessary, but she couldn't concentrate. Albert was rustling through the grocery bags in the trunk and humming a zippy tune. Despite his sweetness, Millie still didn't believe that he really liked her, wouldn't one day look at her open-toed black leather pumps sitting on a floral rug next to their bed and decide that he had had enough. She was a mess, a real big one. He just didn't see it yet.

"Ready, dear?" Mrs. Meibert emerged from the gloom, suited for the occasion in what she called a *slick* outfit of yellow silk with a matching yellow handbag and yellow shoes. Ugh, Millie said to herself. Shoes run in my family. She looked past her mother across the dark backs of the parked cars to the empty street beyond. Something moved in the shadows near a garbage pail. She couldn't quite determine what it was. An opossum? A large rat?

"Did you see that?"

Her mother hadn't. Mrs. Meibert was in too much of a hurry. She scolded Albert for taking so long. What was he doing anyway? He was fussing over his cereal like an old mother hen.

The creature had disappeared. Millie decided that she was tired, strained by the impending event. Her eyes weren't working right.

"I'm so proud of my daughter," Mrs. Meibert said to Albert. Now they were standing together at the end of the car, chatting like old friends.

Millie's stomach fluttered. Her mother was being suspiciously loud. Millie wondered if maybe there were intellectual women nearby.

"I'm so happy Millicent is here. She never gives me a chance to show her off."

Millie slunk out of the car, feeling slightly tipsy as if she had just stepped off a boat. Mrs. Meibert grabbed her arm and led her into the building with Albert trailing two steps behind.

Sitting in the salon for the first ten minutes Millie quieted herself by thinking about all the bills she needed to pay. Then she thought about diamond stud earrings. That's what all the girls in the office wore now. Sharp, hard little squares of glittering rocks that you pinned to your ears. Millie knew where she could put them on layaway.

"Eco rivalry in the environmental system," a few words drifted in. Millie didn't have a problem tuning out the warm-up act, a talk on the "Riparian Universe." The hormonal talk would come next. She could tune out that one, too, if needed. It was easy not to listen at these things.

Albert waved at Millie. Albert had sat on the other side of Millie's mother. Millie could not whisper to him or make eyes at him or hold his comforting hand. He had brought one box of cereal carefully wrapped in a brown bag. She guessed he had brought it in case he got hungry. He'd stuffed it under his seat as if he were on an airplane. Next to her, Millie's mother nodded at the speaker and folded then unfolded her hands. Millie thought she might jump up and throw her arms in the air, "Alleluia," she might say, "Amen to all Riparians," as if she were at a tent revival.

They had been late enough arriving, and Millie had been able to avoid most of the introductions that she dreaded. She imagined them though, her mother standing up tall, introducing Millie to her salon friends in front of Albert: "This is my daughter, she was a poet but she works in advertising now." Actually, Mrs. Meibert hadn't said that. She'd only introduced Millie to one woman, Mrs. Ravencroft, who was slightly stooped and slightly deaf, Millie had guessed because she didn't say anything, or nod, or respond in any way when introduced. But Millie knew that after the lecture when the coffee was served, her mother would make a point of introducing her, and Millie had no idea how to explain the exquisite pain she felt about who she was and what she had become, what she had failed to become.

"This is my daughter," Millie imagined her mother saying. "She'll never be a poet. She has too much stuff."

Millie felt flushed. The flutter in her stomach grew to a sickening flap. Her heart pressed against her chest, and her face heated up like she had a fever. She could not breathe and looked ceiling-ward hoping to force air down her throat, which now prickled with heat. She knew that she could not stay there any longer or she would faint. She could not face the women who would surround her at the end of the lecture pecking like birds at her wounds. Standing up, she stumbled over her mother's legs, pushed Albert's knees aside and nearly tripped on the folding chair. She snagged her new stockings.

"Goodness gracious," her mother said.

"I'm right behind you, Peaches," Albert chimed. A rustling sound followed, and Millie guessed he was trying to pull the cereal bag out from under his chair. Maybe it was stuck. Then Mrs. Meibert said in a loud whisper, "Sit down." Millie didn't have time to think about that. She pushed open the auditorium doors and stepped into the dark parking lot where she stood panting, thinking of how she couldn't face anyone in that room. Now they had seen her for what she was, running away from what she was supposed to be but wasn't because her heart was full of floral prints, angels, and shopping bags.

In a far corner of the parking lot, Millie spied the animal. Barely visible, a shadow darting behind a car, it emerged on the other side, turned, and moved toward her, taking its time, sniffing the pavement, then turned and disappeared behind the next automobile. Millie felt a shiver of recognition—it wasn't an opossum or a raccoon or a giant rat as she had previously thought—it was the dog. The black dog from the garbage dumpster in Jackson. It had followed her here. She knew it was just a coincidence. But given the choice between believing in strangeness or pure logical fact, Millie chose strangeness.

She blinked. What did it mean? At the very least, it was a really bad sign. Like the dead armadillo on her first day of class—in retrospect, she had misinterpreted its meaning, thinking it was good when it was really bad. Well, she wasn't going to misinterpret this one: the dog had appeared just as it had on that night in Jackson when she'd learned the shimmering truth about her mistaken relationship and understood her failure as a poet, even before she'd really begun to try.

The dog stopped next to an old car and stared at her, its ears pricked. Waving feebly, Millie tried to shoo it away.

"Go home," she said. "Leave me alone."

The dog sniffed and licked a nearby bumper. It lifted its leg and peed on a tire. Then without any hesitation, it walked toward her.

It was, maybe, ten yards away—Millie wasn't sure—all she knew was that the dog was approaching fast, yet casually, as if it knew exactly what it was doing, as if it recognized her. Millie braced herself, ready for some cosmic confrontation. Her feet felt rooted to the ground, and she doubted she could run, even if she needed to. Her heart pounding, she glanced at the doors of the salon, fully expecting Albert to burst out, ready to tell her that he was dumping her because he had just met someone new and smart—the Riparian Ph.D. candidate. No, the hormonal studies woman. She was a better fit.

Now the dog walked under the light post, and Millie got her first good look. A terrier mix, black undercoat with wiry silver hairs sticking out, knee-high. This dog was well fed, not a stray. She laughed. What a silly she'd been. It wasn't the same dog after all.

"Here. Here, puppy," she said, even though it wasn't a puppy. She crouched and smiled. The dog glared, black eyes glittering. It seemed to suck air into its mouth, lip instantly curled, and Millie was afraid. Then remembering something she'd learned while working on a dog food campaign—dogs don't like it when you face them head on, smiling, because they think that you are baring your teeth, a sign of aggression. She lowered her head and cooed. The dog sniffed toward her. It stepped close enough for her to pet it. Its coat felt just as she'd imagined, like fine gray wires. It reminded Millie of her own natural hair. It licked her hand and when she stopped petting, it nuzzled her palm, asking for more.

Her shoulders relaxed. Inhaling what felt like a bucket of air, Millie let it seep out from deep inside her, taking away her fear. *I'm so proud of my daughter*, her mother had said to Albert. How unusual! Millie had never heard her mother say that before. She felt as if a small package with her name on it had arrived in the mail. Despite her office job and her bad spending habits, her mother was proud of her and wanted to show her off. That's why she'd wanted Millie to go to the salon so badly. Imagine that! Millie still didn't think she was much to show off but at least her mother thought so. And Albert—he thought she was something special, too, *not bran flakes.*

"Marco," a worried female voice called from down the street. The dog cocked its head and looked attentively. "Marco, where are you?" A second later, a small well-dressed woman with a panicked look on her face appeared on the sidewalk. She held a leash and collar. The dog raced toward her and jumped at her knees. Millie stood up, waving even though she knew the woman wouldn't see her. The dog did though. He turned his head and smiled at her.

In the distance, the red and white light of the grocery store where Albert shopped glowed like an enormous window of stained glass. She took a few hesitant steps toward it, wondering about the possibilities in her life, feeling them for the first time in a long while. Then she walked down the sidewalk toward the store, remembering the comfort of the cereal aisle, hoping Albert would know to find her there.

Robert Herschbach

Infidelity

Same chain, different store—
the order of goods reversed,
light bulbs where the pasta should be,

steaks instead of juice. Checking
for landmarks—bakery, pharmacy—
you're startled by sushi-to-go,

braids of garlic among fat tomatoes,
yellow tomatoes, balloons
tethered to a rack of breads,

the automated downpour
that freshens the greens. Everything
comes from somewhere, small print

on a sticker. Far away, olives are pressed
and locusts whir. Hands you know
nothing of fill tinderbox crates

with clementines, pack the meats,
steer the big rigs through the mountain gap
and all you have to do is choose.

Buy scents and suds, live on
Emerson Ave or Quiet Star Drive,
check the deck for loose nails.

What if you'd married the woman
in aisle five—all that copper hair let loose
in some bedroom not unlike yours . . .

Her toddler swings his legs, points
and keeps repeating something urgently
incomprehensible. The muzak's

some old standard rescored for flute.
Back home, your own family waits,
a tableau turned at a slight angle.

CUBICLES

Conroy, Jonathan 1345

Among the clutter of binders, file folders bulging
with spreadsheets and trimmed with fluorescent orange tabs,
behind the Swingline   stapler he swapped from Skinner's
cube across the hall,   there is a picture of him
sitting with his young daughter   outside the reptile house
at Lincoln Park Zoo. He loved   that day, how she
watched intently as the ostrich   lifted its dirty black wing
to take a pee. *Daddy!*   *It has dinosaur legs!* And he
wondered how he had forgotten the great ancestors of birds,
learned to see pigeons only as rats roosting under el tracks.

Duncan, Arnie 1305

After three years the scar on his chest remains, a puffed worm
among graying chest hair. Mostly, his life is back—racquetball
after work with the guys;   arguments with Liz
over lack of money; his love   of cars, machinery, the purr
of a rebuilt engine. He knows   how changing a part
changes the soul. In his top   left desk drawer, a stash
of Hershey miniatures—scattered   among pens and dried
highlighters—untouched since   his surgery. This new heart
prefers its coffee black, sneaks a cigarette on the drive into work,
listens to soft rock and cracks at the voice of Barry Manilow.

Rosin, Allison 1335

She arranges her desk according to Feng Shui—computer
aligned with a potted lily, forming a diagonal axis to a heated

plate on which she sets her purple   hand-made coffee mug.
A reproduction of Cézanne's   apples delicately pinned
to the blue fabric of the cubical   wall. Every afternoon
Carl knocks on her plastic   nameplate, pops a squat
on the edge of her desk.   Over cinnamon tea they rehash
their fantasy of opening a bed   and breakfast in Cornwall—
how the floors will be slack, the windows drafty; they'll speak
in fake accents, serve gammon & eggs and bad instant coffee.

Wilkinson, Susan   *1315*

Lately, she's depressed afterwards, despite feeling confident
no one saw her getting out his car, walking the extra
three blocks back to work.   His scent lingering on her mouth
used to soothe her, her body   still cold with sweat under
her neatly pressed suit. But   summer grows old, light
slanting new angles through   the window of his garden
apartment—the sounds of children   shouting and running,
spray of a sprinkler and the damp   scent of hose water
drying on the cement. She stares outside as he kisses her
hips, sees a half-deflated beach ball cupping yesterday's rain.

Ritter, Carl   *1320*

8am: arrive, turn on computer, walk down to kitchen while
computer boots up, make coffee, clean out the refrigerator.
8:30am: train new temp. 10am: staff meeting, brief Mr. Weaver
and Arnie about the Cornell account using PowerPoint, make
joke that graphic of stick man holding bomb looks like Skinner.
Noon: lunch with Allison at Sushi Loop, hope she wears royal
blue gypsy skirt. 1pm: check e-mail, voice mail, surf internet.
2pm: go through Cornell file, make provisional decision on
bottom-line offer. 3:30pm: flirt with Allison. 4:30pm: check
e-mail, voice mail, surf internet. 5pm: pack work to take home.

Wilson, Kenneth   *Men's Restroom*

He arrives at 9:30, hiding a hangover behind dark glasses
and a cup of Starbucks, corduroy jacket reeking of cigarettes.
Grabbing the *Sun-Times*, he   makes toward the restroom.
Shitting on the clock, he calls it.   In the stall, his head
spinning, polished black shoes   on both sides, Skinner
on his damned cell phone, talking   up a client. And Ken
thinks about the exchange he has   with his retriever
every morning—*hurry up, Chewbacca,*   *let's go outside*
and do your business; how he can see the dog's breath, his
paws in the frosty grass as he sniffs for just the right spot.

Temporary   *1340*

I cringe at the balding guy training me—his stylish glasses, suit
nicer than I'm able to afford, every joke a reference to Homer
Simpson or Seinfeld. He explains   Modesto is a city
in California, that I should cut   my hair if I want
a real job. After an hour   explaining the transfer
of telephone calls, he   finally leaves me alone
with a pile of filing that takes   all of twenty minutes.
For the rest of the afternoon   I lose his calls, switch
the numbers on his speed dial, use his password to download
teen anal porn into his computer and take a long smoke break.

Bains, Anna   *1310*

She always comes in early to check Mr. Weaver's voice mail,
jot down his messages, file the paperwork from his 6 PM meeting
the night before. She was up   late chatting with sexiguy26,
an artist from San Francisco.   At 10:30, a message on her
HotMail: *so tired this morning,*   *longing 4u, the scent*
of ur hair, nape of ur neck.   His colon/parentheses smile
so stupid among the work day.   Yet at home, laptop resting
on her knees, she feels a twinge   of what she wishes sex
could be—bodies not of bone, over-exerted muscles and sweat;
but pure extensions of the mind: nerve-cell-circuits intertwined.

Gaylord Brewer

DEAD METAPHOR #9: PREGNANT WIFE

Pardon graceless title. We know to you
her girth was luminous, even her most contrary
moods and demands to your ear playful.

How you couldn't stop fondling the moon
of her stomach, measuring a mule bucking
inside, holding seismographic ear against taut skin.

Couldn't stop staring over the frame of your book
even when she asked you, seriously, to stop.
We know you sat on the floor cradling feet,

thought of Jezebel and the Bible, forgave yourself
jumbled similes, ideas in fact a joyful mess.
This was no time to think straight, you thought,

proved it repeatedly through nine months.
Yes, we know the beauty that has overtaken
can't be adequately spoken, sacrifice makes it better,

nothing's shameful in goofiness or prayer.
God would keep her safe, you were certain
He/She would, and that writhing, bellowing,

red-faced monstrosity—so beyond language—
you raise tearfully, humbly to your hospital scrubs,
that's your legacy, raison d'être, the whole

loaded enchilada of life's exquisite purpose,
sapling to your roots. Something like that.
Daddy, daddy, no more tom-foolishness for you.

Here's the digitally edited, fully scored DVD—
syncopated to your lover's contractions—
documenting the whole bloody miracle, just for us.

Interview: Jennifer Merrifield

Jennifer Merrifield's poetry appears in recent or future issues of *Fourteen Hills, Diner, Phoebe, Columbia*, and *Harpur Palate*. An MFA candidate at Virginia Commonwealth University, she is the recipient of the 2006 Columbia Poetry Prize.

Can you tell something about the origin of your poems, how they were written, where, what might have influenced them?

In 6th grade I won a science fair and got to go to Space Camp, where they put us in a Multi-Axis Trainer. I was spun in multiple directions at once, but never felt roller-coaster queasy: I didn't feel like I was moving at all. Paper seems like it's always being held by something— hands, a desk, the screen of a computer—and as important as that touch is, it also negates the page's own gravity because the hands or desk or screen are doing the work of holding it up.

What's holding my poems up is the sense that the speakers are attempting to collect their shifting internal associations, the debris of a moment, because the things that spin are most real and most deserving of immediate attention, and because they're trying to reach out from their orbit as if they were tangible objects that, once studied, will provide the logic necessary to transcend them.

While I realize such internal journeying (and juggling) risks sending some readers to their cereal boxes looking for a magic decoder, the goal of the speaker and the poems is clarity—and a hope that there are readers out there who are compelled by and feel a connection to the speaker's struggle.

How'd you get to be, you know, the way you are?

Like a lot of people, by having a childhood I needed to transcend. It's how people become so multi-layered—like this lasagna from *Southern Living*:

1 pound ground beef
1 medium onion, finely chopped
4 garlic cloves, minced
1 (16-ounce) can stewed tomatoes
2 (6-ounce) cans tomato paste
1 (10 3/4-ounce) can tomato puree
1 tablespoon dried basil
1 teaspoon salt
1 (10-ounce) package dry lasagna noodles
3 cups cottage cheese
2 tablespoons chopped fresh parsley
1 1/2 cups shredded Parmesan cheese
2 large ego events, lightly beaten
1/2 teaspoon salt
1/2 teaspoon pepper
1 pound mozzarella cheese slices

Cook ground beef in a large skillet over medium-high heat, stirring until it crumbles and is no longer pink. Add onion and garlic; cook 3 minutes or until tender; drain. Stir in tomatoes and next 4 ingredients; simmer 30 minutes, stirring occasionally. Cook noodles according to package directions; drain, and set aside.

Combine cottage cheese and next 5 ingredients in a large bowl.

Place half of noodles in a 13- x 9-inch greased baking dish. Spread half of cottage cheese mixture over noodles, and top with half of cheese slices. Spoon meat sauce over cheese. Top with remaining noodles cottage cheese mixture, and cheese slices.

Bake at 375° for 40 minutes. Let stand 10 minutes before appreciating.

What must you do before you can sit down to write?

Make coffee.

What's your cure for writer's block or getting stuck in a story?

I don't believe in writer's block, but I do believe that sometimes we need a little distraction or comfort to get over ourselves and focus on the poem's needs. For distraction, I'll work a puzzle, and when the pieces start flying together, run back to my computer. When I'm feeling really stuck, I make macaroni and cheese.

What is the worst advice anyone has ever given you about writing that you followed before you realized it wasn't working?

My earliest poems were like sonic thickets: language soaked in its own lushness, and the most common feedback I received was people saying that the music was such a pleasure they almost forgot, or almost didn't care, that they couldn't get the same intellectual pleasure of making meaning of it all. After a semester of this, my workshop leader announced that if I were serious about my poetry, I had to strip down the sound and focus on telling a clear, straight narrative of the lyric moment (a clear account of the moment's story)—and only once I accomplished that should I pay any attention to how it felt to the mouth and ears. Maybe this was good advice, but since I came to the notion of narrative believing I would be putting a round peg in a square hole, my poems developed a different sort of murkiness: in trying to pack the space around the peg, it became nearly impossible for a reader to distinguish the poem's focus (the peg) from the tensions and textures that informed it.

What do you think of the idea that more people write poetry or literary fiction than read it?

I think that idea is wonderful and healthy and should be celebrated. When a person takes a painting class or goes to an art store we don't question the breadth of their influences or count how many times they go to galleries and museums; we expect that somewhere along the way that person has been touched by the art and wants to participate in its creation. My father had to work full-time in the coal mines while a full-time law student, but the availability of an MFA allowed me to surround myself with poems and stories and a writing life for three years. I meet lots of people in post offices, convenience stores, Starbucks, etc., and the ecstasy with which they talk about the poems and stories they write, the way they keep turning back to their creativity—even if it's only a few core poems or books that keep them charged—is far more important than whether or not they're reading enough to know the pulse of contemporary literature.

When did you first begin to identify yourself as a writer?

Only recently: one of my Intro to Creative Writing students told me she'd found one of my poems in a journal, copied it, and mailed it home to her mom with a note that said "I'm studying with her!" I was so surprised that I didn't think to ask which poem or journal. Having a student recognize me like that was an important affirmation; especially since I'd thought it was many years and unwritten books away.

Jennifer Merrifield

Breathing Underwater

A daycare kid
tugs his mother's purse strings and drops

down on all fours, skeleton of a leaf

rusted to concrete.

Points at the gutter,
rain missing the mouth to stain a bright bruise. *There?*
There?

In the delivery room red light

swaddling his new body   and as she stares

a box around each year
demanding a little *gratis*
too,
the glare of afternoon blinks and resets:

Septembers full of zeros:

Try again, do-overs, statistic

improbability, it'll all turn out—

Corner to corner, she draws a smile across her mouth.

Jennifer Merrifield

Cold Harbor

i. Siege/Attrition

I knew to curse the dustpan and mop, the days'
irrelevant labors.
Purgatory skins dangling from labeled hooks, but
neat, lined up,
owned. Handled with care, pollution can be worn
naked as the *Hi! I'm* _____
stickers glued to our glass-blown chests. We lie
like snakeskin
and hermit crab husks. Like parades scrolled out
to overstuffed
recliners, the pretend party of live tickertape
on pause.
A season ago the proliferation of cicadas taught
us awe-sucked
breath in every discovery: Here my hand-wrung negligee,
your patched-knee
pants, legs akimbo in a floorless room. *The talk about
talk is the best
it's ever* been . . . In the right light a tear-dropped
onion's undisputed
apology, the peel a flag—so we wave, lay down our
hooks peel back our
clothes before saying *Not now!* then *Maybe tomorrow.* Vain-
glorious we are in
sleep's dumb limb-toss: cherry-sour fruits pushed around
and plucked from
our dinner plates, bushels of sacraments to store beneath
the bed.

ii. Scout and Sentry

A window is open and our house cries elegy:
banged out code, closed

Venetian blinds. Wakes us to speak *over*
and *it's over* for the same different reasons.

House as shadowbox we rearrange in:
puppet-strung, jerked

muscles, the dishes and domestic lifting
veils like Salome. An *I Ching*

on every table: wind
systems of motion, the ghost-read pages.

Pens clicked on and ready to name
each left-behind, for the first time

I can hear your mother
calling you in three-name staccato

and I'm looking for band-aids, a thermometer.
Self-prescribing the triage.

iii. Fortification

An exclamation point is a dot magnified, not in terms of a shape's
revelations under zoom, but as motion amplified through Point A—

So: Sun and birds a warm beaten air to soothe the blood's
      trajectory, Sun and birds a quivered sketch drawn too quick.

Dot as speck looking for its one-way bridge—

From our torn little maps, how to swallow experience from outline?

> Here one rip (no arrow), one briar (no shaft), one bright drop
> (nothing pierced): How to feel touch without imprint?

A hillside will turn its face to the sun, a hillside will sleep under tear-
stained skies. Feet will slip on wet grass. All up motion leads down.

> Tilt windmills for ballast. Avoid mockery and the stuck-out tongue.

> *Hill*: a buckle of earth folded under sky: and here's one more

> blade divisible from grass, one more name for bridge.

> Lexicon-building through deflection—!. !. !. *I may not want to cross yet.*

iv. Treaties

The bricks are all set down, now,
molds taken out back of the homes,
the mallets, golf clubs, tire irons
collected, hate hymns and anthems,
the oppression swept and bundled.
Brutal patience: what bonfires practice,
fiery lover licks and drawn-moth heat.
My carapace cracks nervous before it.
To be carpet-rolled in its metaphor,
to ash my bones in that collective song:
the light of our cigarette tipped bodies
tapped back and trimmed.

Jennifer Merrifield

DEAR SLIPKNOT—

Before you can break, you must collect.

The false start a pathetic misunderstood.

i think i can i think (quick peek) i think (stay down) . . .

So this is the day the ugly girl learns reflection.

Some *chug-chug* for each *hiss-hiss*.

No man is an island but a woman, her hem

raised to the perfect specific is like one:

Her edges ocean blue. Can you hear?

The dinner bell ringing its *clasp* and *slip*.

Jennifer Merrifield

IMAGE IN THE CURRENT

Three state routes feed to a triangle.
Possibilities erode.
Cranes and orange construction mesh
keep us looped a little longer,
the ground come open,
cars kissing up a crooked elbow,
the crawl to come elsewhere
what's missing from home.

Part plus *part* plus *part* and our beginning
resets to threshold. *Mom, the door—*
and the day's dream clicks to god's bike boys—
a fistful of years past
training wheels and *Have you seen*
the hand of God open to hold your life?
and I consider the size of a hand, mine
still closed on the handle not their mouths.

Behind them the wind has started to root
around the pieces, leaves and litter and my aging
unborn kicked off the curb and I'm certain
(in a matter-of-minutes soon)
the lord will come sublime once more
and the miracle will be their pamphlets
on the lawn scattered
to read *End of Construction. Just drive through.*

Jennifer Merrifield

Picnicking in Dorset Park

Most times it's appropriate
to begin with a red-checked cloth

but the willow was modest.
The dry grass meander circled.

With the sun turned up, I slipped
out from my clothes. Left them

to fade in bleached light.
I stepped from my shoes

the trail the stirrups the papered table.
Crouched

down in feathered shelter, I
braided a daffodil noose,

the willow's rest-with-me *shush*,
hung each finger till my knuckles

blanched and the tips throbbed purple.
Sentimentally cool

this shaded air was not a mirage
though I saw my unborn

stretch in a wide checker of light
before setting one pen, one label,

two clinic jars by my clothes
while she waited.

J. Edward Blaisdell

SALVATORE'S

Let me lean like the Tower of Pisa.
Let me fall like the gates of Rome.
Let me lose my innocence and reason.
Let Salvatore's be my home.
—His Highness, Porcelain Statue Jesus Christ III

Holidays and celebrations: they are either for us or against us.

Leida's thirty-third birthday will always remind me that I have no family, no friends, no place to call home. I am, regardless of appearances, broken beyond repair. Three years ago, before I stood on this shelf high above the bar in Salvatore's, I lived at the Van der Tuyns' summer home in Scheveningen, where they stood me in a corner altar with a tiered display of white prayer candles. Whenever the family took a holiday to watch the Netherlands play in the World Cup on the telly, they would inevitably light the candles, turn off the fluorescent overhead, and exclaim, "Oh, how beautiful!" Sometimes they would sing a hymn, but only Valentien, the daughter, sought me on spiritual matters. As a wee girl, she rarely heeded my outstretched arms, overly concerned as she was with teaching the Dalmatian to speak on command, but as she grew older and her body matured, the trials of puberty brought her and her dilemmas increasingly to me. She came to depend on the unfailing acceptance of my arms, my inability to disillusion her with talk. Perhaps in the same way, I came to depend on her juvenile caprice, the precocious lilt of her breasts. In any event, regardless of my attraction, our relationship was set in stone. At night when the others were asleep, she lit several candles and offered me graphic confessions, heartfelt prayers, glistening tears. All I could do was listen, but then, I suppose that's why we got on so well.

She once told me a story about riding her bike to an American soldier's flat after school—this man whom she had just met. They ate dinner, drank beer, undressed, and exorcised her virginity. (Oh, to change, to bleed, to alter one's destiny irrevocably.) I miss my Valentien. She's come to Salvatore's tonight and is sitting there at a table, oblivious to me, lighting a fag, taking her tea with two-year-old Jansen, the boy conceived in that union. Sometimes Jansen sees me, but to him I am simply a statue high above the bar. He may never have a father, but he has Salvatore's.

Below my porcelain feet, I see a shiny copper coffeemaker, and Evelien standing there, steaming up the froth of yet another cappuccino. Her hands are big, wrinkled, but manicured. The rouge on her cheeks is gaudy pink. Before she started bartending here, before she went north to have her "transformation," she, as a man, had been one of the most successful land engineers in Holland. Whenever a Greek shipper needed a barrier beach to protect his fleet, whenever an American developer wanted an island resort where there was no island, he, the man who is now Evelien, bounced sound waves off the ocean floor and found ingenious ways of pumping silt into a pile so high that it breached the surface and sprouted palm trees. In the beginning, his wife tolerated his fancy for women's clothing, sometimes even encouraging it, but as his fetish grew, she turned confrontational, especially when he started mutilating his penis with piercings, refusing her love, denying her persistent requests to swab the angry red lesions with peroxide. "It's infected, my cabbage. It's very bad."

"I know," he said. "Leave it alone."

"Why?"

"I don't want it."

"Why are you doing this!" She beat his hairy chest with her fists.

After saying good-bye to his wife, the man who became Evelien continued his existential plight in the counsel of psychotherapists and doctors who specialized in surgical reassignments. In Utrecht, the swollen mass that had been his penis and scrotum was removed. Surgeons constructed what they termed a "vagina," but it was really just a hole with skin grafts that would never take. He had to dilate the hole continually or else it might close, and it was all but useless in intercourse because the membranes inside were fragile under stress and prone to bleeding. In Amsterdam he received breast implants, hormone treatment, and electrolysis. In Rotterdam he had the brow bone of his skull sanded and the dorsal hump on his nose flattened. Finally, in Maastricht he had his neck lifted, his Adam's apple shaved, and his tummy tucked. On his forty-sixth birthday he changed his birth certificate to read "*Vrouwelijk*" and put it in a scrapbook, right after the photos of his children, who, now grown, refuse to speak to him. Whenever Evelien ruins her mascara with tears, Leida listens for hours.

From my perch centered high above the bar, I see, far across the restaurant, the sweaty, bald head of Maury shining against the orange glow of the fire-brick oven. He spins the pizza-dough disk in the air with the flair of a showman, flattens it on the marble counter, spoons on the tomato sauce. Growing up in the industrial Nowa Huta district of Krakow, Maury shared a bathroom with three steel-working sisters and a Marxist mother. Collectively they hung their gray underwear on the People's radiator. By the time he was thirteen, Maury had developed his sisters' shyness of boys, as well as their attraction to them. During his first week at an all-boys' secondary school on the banks of the Vistula River, his roommate, a lad named Gerik from the cultural, bohemian side of Krakow, kissed Maury on the lips good night. It was a leisurely kiss. It happened only once, but Maury thought about it long afterward. Weeks later, while entering the community shower, he felt a sting on his rump so delightful that again he began to wonder. Towels twirling, the older boys reveled in their ability to intimidate the new students. Pretending to be homosexual, they staged convincing portrayals of bent-over sex in the shower, fellatio in the loo. Initially, Gerik and Maury didn't know whether to run or watch, but by their third year they had become the most adroit dramatists in the shower, surpassing the four-year students in their ability to frighten the first-years, going so far as to incorporate full erections into each scene. It wasn't until Maury came to an inopportune climax that he admitted to himself he was only pretending to pretend.

On graduation, Gerik and Maury moved to Amsterdam to marry and start their graduate education. Over a period of several years they developed a successful counseling firm named Great Minds, offering marital enrichment for same-sex couples. They were featured on the covers of *Expreszo*, *Out Smart*, and *Metro Source*, interviewed on *Barend en van Dorp*, and heralded as the vanguards of Holland's professional gay community—that is, until Gerik died of a heroin overdose and Maury had himself committed to the psychiatric hospital De Kijvelanden. Great Minds went bankrupt. Now whenever Maury suffers a breakup, Madam Leida doubles his work, forcing him to stay within the walls of Salvatore's.

The day that Leida saw me at the Van der Tuyns' summer house, Mr. Van der Tuyn lit the candles, turned off the lights, and watched her exclaim, "Oh, how miserable!" And since it was her thirty-third birthday, he wrapped me in tissue paper, tied a ribbon around my waist, and placed me in her hands. (I didn't see Valentien for a year.) For this year's thirty-third birthday, which officially starts in ten minutes, Leida wears a shoulderless black blouse that matches her cropped hair and high heels. That's her there, with the brass hoop earrings, sitting with two new customers, husband and wife, showing them pictures of her sunbathing at a nude resort near Cannes. Leida hates cooking, but she enjoys being the mistress of a restaurant that has a cult following. If Salvatore's were a rock band, she would be the lead singer. The regulars enjoy her food, but they come more to see her next costume and hairstyle, to watch her flatter old men in the language of their choice— Dutch, German, Italian, French, or English. She has a talent for rising from her table in a posture that exposes maximum cleavage, for treating each returning customer as a prodigal child. On the weekdays, if the dining room becomes too quiet, she blares Puccini over the speakers, lip-synchs, and seats customers as if she were Maria Callas. Then, too, if she needs a distraction for, say, a barfing beagle under the table, her laughter will rise to a volume and pitch suggestive of a bone-melting orgasm, inciting the women to laugh, half embarrassed, and the men to laugh, half aroused. Leida enjoys introducing lone customers to each other. She sits them at adjacent tables, serves them free wine, starts a three-way conversation, and giggles as they go from proper strangers to wedding-day drunks. Her affinity for such antics originated, I assume, in adolescence.

Having more than the normal measure of confidence allotted to a teenager, Leida left her parents' home at sixteen and never returned. She did not rebel against them, nor was she preoccupied with finding herself in an epiphanic moment induced by coffee and the old, rain-shiny streets of Europe. Rather, she was acting on the belief that she possessed a clarity of thought and a passion for life unique in their ability to change others. With ninety-five guilders, a voluminous hemp purse, and a winning smile, she left home with an acute enrichment of love in her veins, as if she contained the only known antibody proven to fortify the human condition against all forms of subdued dreams and failed relationships. In the letter that she left her parents, she said simply, "I want to make people happy."

On a cold, rainy Queen's Day she took the train to Paris and, within a short walk of the station, found work as a waitress at Le Jardin D'Artemis, a candlelit three-room, midscale restaurant of oaken beams and exposed brick. There she acquired an eclectic mix of regulars, one of whom, a well-to-do middle-aged man with a dark tan and glossy fingernails, invited her to see the Bastille Day fireworks show from the captain's seat of his Beneteau yacht. As she stared into the sky and watched the loud explosions spatter the night with blue-white-red, she noticed a sudden sense of sleepiness, and her lips going numb. Was she really this drunk after a few sips of beer? Or was there another reason for the fireworks blurring, the bottle slipping from her hand? Without knowing why, she fell forward and slammed her nose into the safety-grip steps. Even more confusing, she saw a two-headed man sit next to her and laugh like a white-eyed cannibal. She saw other men, too, naked (except for jewelry), multi-armed, dancing around her like Hindu gods. They undressed her and took turns lying between her legs, making her feel as if she were being tickled to death. They smacked her rather playfully, then beat her in what seemed a much harsher manner. With her eyes swollen shut, she could feel herself being hoisted into the air by her underarms and ankles, being swung to and fro to the throng's drunken count of "*un, deux, trois,*" and thrown into the Seine. The water rushed over her head, into her lungs, and that's when she first began to suspect that bad luck—the irrevocable type—might have found her.

Of course, I have never been so fortunate as to be so obviously broken—gang-raped and thrown in a river. I will never have my first and only lover convulse and die in my arms, as Maury had. A soldier will never plant a child in my womb and disappear, as happened with Valentien. Nor will my appearance ever reflect the alienation of an aging transsexual, like Evelien's. If I were able, I would hurl myself down upon the marble top of this bar and let Leida collect the pieces.

Simon is "the American." He's the one in the blue polo shirt, sitting at the family table, sharing a liter of merlot with Fred. He's eating the pizza that Maury just baked and talking about the football game with Manchester United. Unlike his fraternal twin brother who had modeled in fashion magazines and dated cheerleaders, Simon grew up in a genetic limbo, on the verge of handsome, but not quite. "The Beautiful Girl," in his mind, had never been out of reach. He'd plan and work, and when his efforts inevitably failed, he seldom sought comfort from the common girls he could readily have. No, Simon wanted The Beautiful Girl, her muscular legs beckoning underneath the mini skirt, her capable lips, easy smile, the loose unbuttoned V in her school uniform, her tweezed symmetrical eyebrows that could cut independently of the other. He had always felt entitled to such things. He had always been lonely.

While studying international affairs in college, Simon interned abroad at the Hague and eventually found work with the American Department of Defense in Brunssum. During his annual holiday visit to Tennessee, on the eve, actually, of his flight back to Europe, he happened upon a Beautiful Girl he had known several years prior, when she had been too young, too Baptist, for them to explore a pre-marital attraction. But now that Kinsey Strout was twenty-one and chain-smoking in a pub, Simon smiled at his good fortune and greeted her with a simple "Hello, Kinsey." Initially she did not recognize him, but then she said, "Oh my fucking God," and as they melted into a hug, their former taboos tasted like aged wine. When the pub closed at midnight, she drove him to an art studio near the community college she attended. There they sat on a paint-stained couch, drank coffee, and talked for hours among student sculptures and paintings, a portrait of her boyfriend, Smitty. "It's almost three," she said, her thigh pressed against his. "When do you want me to take you to your car?"

"Could we go back to your place?"

A gentle smile. She looked at the floor.

"Or we can crash here."

"I want to." She looked at him. "But I can't." She pointed at the portrait of Smitty.

"I'm going back to Europe. It's not like I'm going to interfere."

"You don't have to face him tomorrow, I do."

"It's just one night. Our present to each other. We'll take it with us wherever we go."

She looked at him a long time and shook her head.

He moved closer to her. "At least a kiss."

She stood from the couch. "Yeah and then we're doing it all anyway. Look Simon, no, I'm not going to sleep with you. That's it."

"Okay."

"Who knows what the future holds. I may come to see you. But don't expect it. I can't promise you anything." She sat on a stool in front of an easel.

"Maybe you should take me to my car."

She attached a sheet of paper to the clip at the top of the easel. "But I would like to draw you. Without your clothes on."

"You want me to strip?"

"There's a changing room through that door. Come out and stand on the platform."

"What if I'm aroused?"

"I'm aroused." She took the top off a box of charcoals.

"Visibly aroused."

"That's fine, Simon. But you can't come near me. Ten feet minimum."

Leaving his coat on the couch, he got up and looked through the door that led to the changing room. A red exit sign illuminated an otherwise dark hallway. He walked down the hall and stood between the door of the changing room and the exit. One door led to an erotic experience, the other, perhaps to something more. Without hesitation, Simon pushed open the exit door. The air was cold against his arms. He jogged to the nearest gas station and called a cab.

A few days later, when he e-mailed her from the Netherlands, she responded with an equally long explanation. Like Simon, Kinsey was confused, but quite possibly on the verge of love. After several weeks of intimate confessions, they agreed to wait until they could see each other again, to see if it was as real as it seemed. During that time, when Simon dined at Salvatore's, he sat alone at the table to my right, the one wedged between the end of the bar and the wall. Occasionally he talked to Evelien, but more often he liked to drink slowly and luxuriate in a refined solitude. He seemed content to stare at the oils and photographs hanging from the walls, to cherish his thoughts, whatever they may have been. But the following Christmas, when he returned to the States for his annual holiday, Kinsey's mobile number was no longer in service. He called her parents' house and introduced himself. Kinsey's father gave him a new phone number, but Simon didn't recognize the area code.

"She and Doug live in Atlanta."

"Doug?"

"Her husband, he has a church down there. We're expecting them in tomorrow. Do you want me to give her a message?"

"A message."

"She'll remember you won't she?"

"No, no message. Thank you very much."

Now, whenever Simon dines at Salvatore's, he sits at the family table.

With a few customers remaining in the restaurant, Leida fills three pitchers of beer on a tray and hoists it above her shoulder. In a series of graceful movements, she weaves through the tables and dumps the tray on Valentien's shoulders. "Oh! Sorry! Sorry, Valentien. I'm so sorry."

Valentien stands, beer dripping from her fingers. Two-year-old Jansen inhales for a count of five and blares like a rooftop siren. Leida lifts the child and jostles him into her breasts. He screams louder.

"Evelien!" Leida puts the boy on her hip and bounces. "Evelien!"

Evelien hurries from behind the bar and starts to take the child, but Leida shakes her head and points to Valentien. "Find her something to wear. Take her upstairs. Find her something for the party."

Jansen continues to scream. Valentien reaches for him.

"No, no, no," Leida says. "Go upstairs. Evelien is a fashionable woman."

Evelien smiles.

Valentien frowns, but she follows Evelien.

Leida bounces Jansen on her thigh. "Don't be sad." *Bounce. Bounce.* "Leida will make you better." *Bounce. Bounce.*

As soon as Valentien leaves, Leida strides toward the family table and dollops Jansen in Simon's lap. Simon is terrified. Fred laughs.

"No." Simon lifts Jansen. "Here."

Leida shakes her head. "You are good with children."

"I've never—"

"I must clean." Leida leaves the table and goes behind the bar to get a mop.

Jansen screams so loud that Simon closes his eyes.

Fred eats his penne and scampi and laughs.

Although he currently runs a small windshield-repair business, Fred tended bar for five years at the Escape in the Rembrandtplein of Amsterdam. It was there that he met Natascha, the real-estate agent who is the mother of their eight-year-old daughter. On the day that Natascha told him she was pregnant Fred hugged her and proposed.

"I am a complex cluster of traits," she said. "I need a variety of men to satisfy my desires."

"What do you mean?"

If Natascha were a book, she would be a leather-bound, gilded-paged volume of Victorian erotica. If she were a car, she would be a 1927 Bentley with a 2008 Ferrari engine. If she were an animal, she would be a sea dragon dwelling in the deepest canyons of the ocean, attracting friends with her light, then eating them. Fred, poor soul, was simply Fred. If he were an animal, he would still be Fred. During the pregnancy and several years thereafter, Natascha seemed so preoccupied with motherhood that her "complex cluster of traits" remained dormant, like spores of bacilli encased under meters of arctic ice. Fred thought that if he continued to love her and make family life more appealing than the variety of men she had envisioned, Natascha would realize that marriage offered greater opportunities for fulfillment. He was so sure that she had changed, he bought her a classic solitaire, put it in a bedside drawer, and presented it to her in a navy velvet box while they were still interlocked, recovering from orgasm.

"Don't ask me again."

His penis shrank inside her. "I don't understand."

"I said I wasn't the type."

"But you *are*. We're more married than a lot of couples."

"We're not."

"We're parents." He pulled himself up from her. "We sleep in the same bed each night. I've been faithful to you, and you've been faithful to—"

Natascha pushed him from between her legs and climbed out of the bed, pulling the sheet with her.

Fred sat on the edge of the bed. "You're seeing someone?"

"I told you I would."

"When do you—"

"When you're mixing martinis."

Fred stood, the condom hanging half off him. "Do you know how many women I could have fucked?"

"You should have."

"Why?"

"Then don't, I don't care." She went into the loo and locked the door.

He put his face near the door. "You're a cold bitch."

"I told you from the beginning."

"Do you love the other guy?"

"Some of them."

"How many?"

"Stop it, Fred, just stop it."

Fred shouldered the door and broke the lock. "You're the one who's fucking the neighborhood."

She rose from the toilet and flushed.

Fred yanked the pendent condom and threw it in the toilet. "Do you love me more than them?"

She sidled around him and went into the bedroom. "Sometimes."

"Then *you* stop it," he said.

"No."

"I'll leave."

"Then leave." Natascha opened the top drawer of her dresser—her panty drawer—removed a neon orange thong, and stepped into it, her bottom facing him. "You're not going to dictate my life."

"I'm not dictating! I ask of you what I ask of myself."

"I told you from the beginning."

"You were pregnant and—"

"I was honest!"

She was honest. She was sensual, discreet, and smart and had no shortage of men to choose from. No lover ever knew of the others' existence. In retaliation, Fred started sleeping with a woman he had met while tending bar. He received a call at four in the morning.

"Who was that?" Natascha sat up in bed.

"No one." He rolled over, turning his back to her.

"What did she want?"

"Nothing."

"Good night, Fred."

"Night."

"I love you."

Fred said nothing.

"I said, I love you."

"Love you too."

In theory, Natascha respected Fred's right to sleep with other women, as long as he was smart about it, but like many people, Fred believed that rationing his love made it more valuable. Consequently, whatever affection he gave to this new woman in his life, he withdrew from Natascha. He stopped calling her at work and asking her opinion. He stopped telling her where he was going and how late he would be. These actions, however, didn't hurt her. It was his intent to hurt that caused the pain.

After the night of the phone call, Natascha brought home one of her own lovers, an appraiser from the real-estate agency where she worked. She introduced him and politely asked Fred if he would mind sleeping on the couch when he returned from tending bar. Smiling, Fred punched the man, dragged him out of the apartment, and threw him down the stairs. He then came back into the apartment, washed his hands, and took his gym bag out of the closet.

"Where are you going?" Natascha asked.

"To think."

He would not return for eleven weeks. In Lucerne, after running out of money, he grew a beard, slept on benches, and lost a toe to frost-bite. In Paris, while drinking under the Bir-Hakeim Bridge, he heard laughter, then a splash, and saw Leida floating in the river.

"You have a lovely wife," Simon once told Fred. "Where did you find her?"

"In the river."

Simon laughed. Evelien and Maury laughed. And Leida, she laughed the most.

Simon allows little Jansen to run and wail and search for his mother until he is so tired that he reaches out his arms. Simon lifts him, and together they visit Maury and help him sprinkle cheese in a pan of lasagna. They visit Evelien and help her take wine goblets out of the dishwasher. Simon rolls an empty pinot noir bottle down the glass chute; it makes a loud klink. "All gone." He looks around for other means to entertain Jansen and, to my surprise, points to me.

"Who's that?"

Jansen looks at Simon and smiles.

Simon walks toward me, lifts me down from the shelf, and lets Jansen touch my cool, smooth surface. "Who's that?"

Jansen looks at me. "*Gaaaaaaah!*" He pushes me from Simon's hands.

"Jansen!"

I tumble in the air.

My destiny.

My salvation.

I shatter on Evelien's step stool, onto the floor. My head is in one piece, but I have lost every part of me except my upper torso and one arm.

"No problem." Leida comes around the bar, picks me up, and sets me on the marble counter. From here I am almost level with the family table. Leida grabs a broom and sweeps my remains into a pile.

Taking his seat across from Fred, Simon lifts Jansen into the air, making a swooshing sound with his mouth. Jansen smiles just as Valentien comes into my view wearing an accordion-pleated olive skirt and a blouse with a plunging neckline.

"Wow," Fred says.

Valentien pulls an antique chair next to Simon's and waves to her son. Jansen opens and closes his hand and puts his head on Simon's chest.

"He's tired," Simon says.

"It's normal," says Valentien.

"You look nice."

"Thank you." She smiles. "Leida is very clumsy."

Simon rubs Jansen on the back. "No she's not." He rubs Jansen and rocks.

As Puccini's *Nessun Dorma* plays over the speakers, Leida tosses my shattered pieces into the rubbage bin, picks up the remnant of my former self, and sits at the family table. "Okay, everybody!" Maury slides the bolt of the front door. He pulls an antique chair to the other side of Leida, and kisses her on the cheek. Evelien comes out of the kitchen with cake of flaming candles. She sets it in the center of the table. The lights go out.

I was the third statue to occupy Salvatore's top shelf, the others being too perfect, I suppose, for her taste. Unlike them, I had no sacred heart painted on my chest, no burgundy cape on my shoulders, no tassels of gold. I was to stand as the sole symbol of Salvatore's while Leida flirted with the customers and Evelien steamed espresso, while Maury baked pizzas and Fred drank with Simon.

"Ahh!" With a seductive smile, Leida inserts my broken body into the top of the cake. I am up to my elbow in chocolate icing. She claps her hands. "Hooray!"

Fred rolls his eyes.

Simon cuddles Jansen.

Valentien blows a kiss to Jansen, or perhaps to Simon.

In a rich baritone voice, Evelien begins to sing "Happy Birthday," and while the others enjoin from around the family table, I sit quietly and try to maintain my composure.

Erin M. Bertram

[Mesmerist]

Find me fractured, head on one shoulder like a colt,

composure just one more heady illusion. An apple beneath
my top hat to remember the weight of sin, cape tied

too tight for austerity's sake—a showman's finely taut face.

If, sleight of hand, quick flick of the wrist, a gesture fails
to impress, what—abrupt? meticulous?—move next to call my own?

Slats comprise the box, 2 x 4's just for show. Evenings

> I saw her in half, mornings she expects reassembly
>
> with a steady hand. So I acquiesce, spent of tricks
>
> from the night before. What appears magic (materialization,
>
> complete & total dismissal) so many lights, pipe smoke,
>
> one more card tucked neatly up the sleeve. When I meet
> my face in the glass, rouge smeared, gloves sawdust
>
> sallow, I am the lion's mane, I am the vanishing dove.

Erin M. Bertram

[ON THE FLEDGE]

Auguries staid & atonal, which is to say plausible, which is to say true,

if only for a brief moment passing. In the leather case, compass,

shotgun, SLR. Expressions pliant as wheat sheaves combed over &

over in the field. We stood vigil over graceless pink muscle, one wing

buzzing—crazed, askew—as the other held its place, locked pocket of

feather & damp. Sunken head, still beak, still moist down. S. called it

'she,' praised its necessary hopping for lack of a better, more

respectable, less compromised, trait. Skein alighting overhead.

Shallow puddle tossing back

the sun's one flaming eye. Saddle

polished in the barn, hornets convene in a musty corner, a

convergence of rotted-out beams. S. offered her flecks of corn,

stroked her spent & arcing, arcing back with shadows. For an hour

we watched what was left make its way out from the body's walls.

Wind collected through & through trees, & at times she fluttered,

mime to the tearing around her. S. scooped her up, held high against

the bruise of sky, one first & final blend with the air, gessoed there,

however passing. The flagrant permanence of stars, her, beneath,

cautious, unwitting, suspended.

Erin M. Bertram

[Sink Slowly The Earth]

Saddle bags swollen with goods.

> *In a past life I was a messenger, smelling of tobacco & manure.*

Swimming pool full of floundering children.

> *Water wings.*

Hotel of flies, honeycomb in every closet.

> *Keep searching, children. I was told all the closets.*

The river pushes east to west & I can't get out of bed.

> *Here I speak for a friend. Her pills are a sieve, herself held in the basin.*

Stains on the walls, our clothes, our hands, in our hair.

> *What are you if not dirty?*

Forgiveness in all the wrong places.

> *Here, you can buy an oxygen hit for the price of a beer.*

Jack & Ginger, White Russian, Red-headed Slut, Black & Tan.

> *We sip drinks that sound like people.*

Glass emptied of ice & hue, what is left the heft of a vessel.

> *Blown earnest into being, the white flame viscous.*

You are that vessel.

> *Yes. You are that vessel.*

If the river ran backward, then she could get up.

> *Night & day would eclipse one another, & all the world would blind.*

Know your colors, your apostles, your sins, & your saints.

> *Eat your Sunday brunch with fists.*

Scrounge for bread as minnows to calves.

> *They're not curious, they're hungry.*

In the air, manure & tobacco, hanging.

> *Soon after scent, the mouth, as well, fills.*

This is my rifle, this is my gun—

> *Your nails haven't been cut for days.*

Beyond the camp, wind whipping its own back.

Laurel Smith

UNDISCOVERED LETTER,
V. WOOLF TO K. MANSFIELD

October 1928

Katherine,

On what would be your fortieth birthday,
They want a public "memoir" of you. They
Have offered to pay. But they don't understand
My details of the rain, the acorns that litter
The walk, the sound of the press downstairs.
Why, I can imagine the editor thinking,
Doesn't Mrs. Woolf start with some allusion
Then get on with the gossip?
But the editor met you once only
And imagines Murry—your meticulous keeper—
Is destined for a Chair at Cambridge.
Even with my desire to have
    Virginia Woolf, author
In print everywhere, it's no use to plot
Pennies by the word on such an assignment as this.

I miss your letters, your blunt reviews.
I cannot stop thinking of what you have missed,
What you would like to see yourself:
The gold leaves and purple asters, the grey smoke from
A cigarette, Leonard's muddy boots in the hall.

I Met A Guy

I once met a guy who was thirty-five years old but didn't have a single one of his teeth left. He'd hold his hand in front of his face if, for some reason, he thought about his dental plates. We were both shaving one night, leaning against the sinks. "How'd you lose all your teeth, man?" I made two fists, raised my eyebrows.

"No, no," he said. "I'm a drinker. There's a lot of falling down involved. And I didn't own a toothbrush, see, not really, until I came here."

When he said *here*, he meant Plainfield, the prison where I spent four years after I turned twenty. Four years is not much in the big scheme of things, of course, unless you look on it as just the down payment for a whole lifetime that's going to be spent locked up, a little bit here and a little bit there. A lot of guys I met were doing life on the installment plan, as they say.

I've done some bad things in my life, but who hasn't? Me, I've never done anything bad except when I was drunk or high, and I think that says something, though maybe not much. We can't all be gentle, happy drunks.

The most famous resident ever at Plainfield was Mike Tyson, though he was long gone by the time I got there. I met a guy who said Tyson once asked him: "If we shot a rocket to the sun at night, would it burn up?" I used to wonder how someone so rich and famous could ever feel like he had to go rape some girl, but now I know. There are a lot of stupid people in this world and Mike Tyson is probably one of the stupidest. I mean: Jesus fucking Christ!

My brother hates it when I start a story, "I met this guy . . ." because he knows I mean, "I met this guy in prison . . ." and I'm just trying to be polite around his kids. It makes my brother uncomfortable to hear me look back on that time and laugh. Like maybe he thinks I might for some reason want to go back to prison, or I'm going to take his kids there someday. I'm going to paint such a pretty picture of all these dead-end jackasses I know, such a fairy tale that my memories will spread like perfume over the dinner table and his little boy is going to want to lose his teeth and spend a few years with empty pockets himself, seeing cars only distantly through barb wire. And his two little girls are going to fall in love with men like me who beat them and get locked up for years at a time.

But shit, that's my life. You can't wish your life away.

I met a guy who had so many tattoos that, in the showers, he looked like the Incredible Hulk, all green and shit. His right forearm was fucked up; he'd done it himself when he was fifteen, left-handed with homemade ink, and it looked like a ransom note, on fire, smeared, coming apart in smoke. The rest was professional. All in all, his skin was one great cursive signature, half barb wire and half ribbon. He had a couple skulls in green. And on one shoulder he had a skeleton sitting with its knees in front of its jaw, its hands clutched above its head. That skeleton looked scared, but most of his skulls looked like burnt-out houses. He had a blue woman with enormous tits on the inside of one leg. I saw this in the shower and he offered me a closer look but I declined. Around his throat, it looked like tooth-marks, but it was calligraphy that said, *The Love Bitch*. When I asked him what that meant, he shrugged. Then finally: "Just what it says."

There was this boy, Thomas, who was twenty-two. If he'd been a white guy that age, he'd have had a beard and mustache, trying to look older, because a baby girl face doesn't do you favors in prison, but it takes a lot for a brother that age to grow a good beard. Thomas kept himself clean. Though it's also true that he would suck cock at a moment's notice.

Thomas wasn't a lady like a couple of the men who worked in the barber shop. They were loud and fluttery, all the time scolding people for bad manners and laughing their high-pitched birdsongs about nothing. That kind of laughter was like a lot of things in prison. It didn't really say, *I'm happy*, though these ladies were happier than they had a right to be. No, when they laughed so loudly, it said the same thing as eighty percent of what I heard in prison. It said: *look at me, look at me.*

In prison, some guys will bet on anything. One guy, Bones—skinny guy, real name Jones, but completely meatless, looked like broken broomsticks, his arms and legs just hanging from the throw-pillow of his chest—he would bet on the weather. I heard that, in county lockup, you could pick a name and Bones would bet you whether it would be on an odd or even page in the phone book. He was like a lot of guys that way. If you didn't want to bet instant soups or your commissary, he'd bet you for envelopes. Every month you got four envelopes free from the state and of course you could buy a box of fifty on commissary—he'd bet you for them. Bones didn't even write letters. He just wanted to win something. Anything.

For a while, Bones and some other people were betting on spiders. They'd catch spiders and make them fight on top of a book or something. The spiders never lasted too long; you'd never have a returning champion more than three or four fights because they were always tearing each other's legs off. But then Virgil Wright, who didn't even bet on the spider fights, found a millipede and put it in, and the millipede killed first one spider, then another, and so on—for two days, until no one had any spiders left or they wouldn't put them down to fight. "It's not fair," said Bones.

"Get your own damn millipede," Virgil said, but when no one did, he flushed his down the toilet. I told him that wasn't very fair either. The millipede had been a good soldier. Virgil just shrugged. "It ain't like it's my fucking dog," he said.

Sometimes I think about Campbell Prossey, how he was the poster boy for the phrase "Chester the Molester" because he was so old and rickety, with eyes that looked like they were about to fall out of his wrinkled head. When he talked, he talked about his time in Germany in the army, which no young person wanted to hear, and in the months I knew him, I never saw him without a pair of white cotton gloves. The gloves were graying at the fingertips, the knuckles and seams frayed and coming apart. He'd write letters with those gloves on, eat dinner like that—he went to bed with his sheet in those little white fists. He said he was afraid of germs; he looked like a sick Disney character. When I heard about him getting cut up, I imagined his bunkmate in the two-man cell, some young guy, climbing onto Campbell Prossey's chest in the dark morning, putting a knee on each shoulder, and cutting a ring on the old man's throat with a sharpened piece of scrap metal. I heard that Prossey's T-shirt and chin were red like Hawaiian Punch. I imagined the old guy screaming and moaning and no one coming to help him for long minutes, then an officer, who no doubt stood in the doorway and radioed for help because he wasn't going to jump on that knife. Prossey was lucky he didn't need any CPR or anything. I'd seen some officers joking after their annual CPR training. "Here's how I'd give an inmate mouth to mouth," one said. He put his foot onto his friend's and whispered: *"Hey, get up, get up."*

My brother and my sister-in-law cover their ears when I tell a story about Campbell Prossey; they don't want to hear it. They want to hear about how I've changed and how I'm not drinking anymore, and all that may be true but what's the point of talking about it? What's the point of talking about something you're *not* doing? I try to think a bit more about other people now; that's a decision I made. I've been told it was time. But when I think about the people I know, nobody wants to hear it. Where's the love, I think? Where's your love for Campbell Prossey?

Everyone at Plainfield had pictures of home, but one guy—everyone called him Red Dog on account of a sunburn made him look like the dog on the beer bottle—Red Dog had a dozen pictures of his old girlfriend and his car and whenever he wrote a letter, he'd arrange the photos around the edge of the Rec table and then lean over his paper surrounded by them all. "You writing a letter to her or the car?" I asked him.

"Her," he said, holding one photo up.

She was in a swimsuit, holding a garden hose over the hood of a Bondo-colored Lincoln. "Hey," I said, "can I have this?"

He took it from my fingers. "You're lucky I let you look at it."

And, looking at the picture, this twenty-year-old girl with long, straight hair and a sunburn that matched his, a car that never got more than maybe fifteen miles to the gallon even back when it rolled off the line, I imagined the two of them, two sunburns, and thought they'd look like peppermint sticks once they had their clothes off. I thought about how long it had been since I'd owned a set of keys, let alone a car, and I asked Red Dog how long he'd been in and how long he had to go. He told me. And then I didn't feel so bad because I knew Jody—that's what we called our so-called best friends, the guys who were still outside—Jody would come along sooner or later, a shoulder to cry on, and then, the girl wouldn't be sending any more letters to Red Dog, his car would be gone too, no one paying the insurance, or some uncle using it for parts, and eventually, all he'd have left were these pictures.

My brother doesn't want to hear about this. He says, "My God, can't you just forget about it?" And I think: the way you did me, when I was locked up? The way you sent me one birthday card the four years I was there? The way you and your wife had your little girls and you didn't send me a picture till they were three months old? You think it's a good thing to forget about people?

I knew a guy called Johnson; Johnson was forty-years old, always chuckling, always pleasant, with a thin afro that left gray hairs on the bathroom sink when he brushed his scalp. I was in the visiting room when Johnson started crying because his mother said she was never coming back to see him anymore. "I'm tired," she said. "I'm sixty-three years old. You come out and see *me* for a change."

Johnson leaned forward. "I'm trying, Mama. I'm trying."

"Now, you been in and out, *trying*, for thirty years, baby." The old woman tilted her gray head. "You know we don't even set a place for you at Thanksgiving anymore? What's a man your age gettin' in trouble for over cigarettes? If they say not to have tobacco, you don't keep it, baby. It's that simple."

And Johnson started crying—right there in the busy crowd of people at their tiny plastic tables, their plastic lawn chairs, and the opened bags of Chee-tos and empty cans of pop. A forty-year-old man who'd spent Christmas Day watching other people talk on the phone— I saw him cry. Little wet stars appeared on the concrete floor. I wanted to reach over and tell her: it's not his fault; he only said the tobacco was his 'cause Willie Wee just had five weeks to go. And Willie, that asshole, was getting a six-month time cut for substance abuse class, but he would have lost that cut if he'd been caught with tobacco. Johnson was teaching Willie chess, and wouldn't be free for at least eight more years anyway so he said the smokes were his.

But I didn't say anything to Johnson's mom because it wasn't my place. Willie Wee wore spotless white basketball shoes and smelled of Polo and if it had been up to me, he could have spent the rest of his life in that place. Johnson had given him six months, but I knew it was the kind of thing that could never, ever, be paid back and so, for that reason, it was stupid.

My brother asked me one night in the garage: "You really miss those guys? That why you talk about them?"

And I said, "No, I don't miss them. You don't get it at all. You think I love these guys? You think that's why I talk about them? Listen, nobody loves these guys. Nobody. Everybody forgets them."

My brother put his beer down on the hood of his car. Stared at it.

"But I'm different," I said. "I'm going to be different. I am."

My brother didn't say anything. He didn't even ask me what I was talking about or who I thought I was.

I'd known these men for months and years at a time. Some of them I met when my family wasn't speaking to me, when I didn't have five square feet to myself. I showered with these men; we slept in the same room, ate twelve to a table. All of us were given the same mashed potatoes and cigar-colored gravy. During lockdowns, we ate identical baloney sandwiches three meals a day. I'd never seen a Mexican cry until one time we were locked down for three days and the last day he opened his brown bag and saw another white bread sandwich with yellow mustard. One of his friends told me that guy never ate bread before, on the outside. Only tortillas. But you never really know anybody because, looking back on it, I can't even remember these guys' real names. I only know what we called each other. The names we made up. And half the time I can't even remember those—I just remember faces.

Last Christmas, I was in Kroger's with my sister-in-law and her two little girls. I had the cart and I saw Bones at one register. And I didn't think: when did he get out, is he still gambling now, is he one of the white guys who was in for rape or drinking or was it crank? I thought about my brother's two little girls, who were hanging onto the grocery cart, their ankles hitting the floor, and I thought only: Bones— please, God, don't let him see me.

Contributors' Notes

Erin M. Bertram is a graduate fellow in the MFA program at Washington University in St. Louis. Her poems have appeared or are forthcoming in *Bloom*, *Columbia Poetry Review*, *TYPO*, and *Word For/Word*, and in *Combatives* with Sarah Lilius. She reads for *River Styx* and freelances for *The Vital Voice*. Her chapbook *Alluvium* is forthcoming from dancing girl press (2007).

J. Edward Blaisdell graduated from Emory & Henry College and lived in the Netherlands for four years. He currently resides in Nashville, where he is finishing his first novel.

Gaylord Brewer is a professor at Middle Tennessee State University, where he edits *Poems & Plays*. His most recent book of poetry, a collection of apologias, is *Let Me Explain* (Iris Press, 2006). His work also appears in *Best American Poetry 2006*.

Garrett J. Brown's poems have most recently appeared in the *American Poetry Journal*, *Urbanite Baltimore*, and the *Ledge*. In 2000, he won a Creative Writing Fellowship from the School of the Art Institute of Chicago, where he graduated with his MFA in Creative Writing. His book-length manuscript, *Manna Sifting*, was runner-up in the 2003 Maryland Emerging Voices competition and he won the Poetry Center of Chicago's 2005 Juried Reading Contest, judged by Jorie Graham. Garrett's chapbook, *Panning the Sky*, was published in 2003 and is available from Pudding House Publications.

Mairéad Byrne is an associate professor of English at Rhode Island School of Design in Providence. Recent poetry publications include a collection, *Nelson & The Huruburu Bird* (Wild Honey Press, 2003), three chapbooks: *An Educated Heart* (Palm Press ,2005), *Vivas* (Wild Honey Press 2005), *Kalends* (Belladonna*, 2005); and a talk: *Some Differences Between Poetry & Standup* (UbuWeb, 2005).

Mary Cisper lives in northern New Mexico where she has labored as a chemist and found joy in poetry and art. "Pandora Sets the Table" is her third published poem. She is grateful to all her teachers.

Andy Cox lives in St. Louis with his wife Terry and daughter Rachel. His manuscript, *The Equation That Explains Everything*, was a finalist in Four Way Book's Intro Prize. Poems have appeared recently in *Sentence* and *River Styx*.

Christopher Davis's third collection of poetry, *A History of the Only War*, was published in 2005 by Four Way Books. New work recently appears in *Interim, Court Green, Crazyhorse,* and *Colorado Review*.

Gloria Garfunkel is a graduate student of fiction in the low-residency MFA program at Bennington College in Vermont. She graduated Barnard College with a major in art history and Harvard University with a Ph.D. in psychology and social relations. She lives within walking distance of Harvard Square, has a psychotherapy practice, a professorial husband, two adolescent sons, and three quirky cats. She has never been able to choose between art, psychology, and literature, so she is mastering all three in what she hopes will be twenty-year successions. "Birds of Prayer" is her first published story.

Sarah Giannobile (Cover Art) earned her BFA from Webster University and her MA and MFA from Fontbonne University. She also received a scholarship to attend the Anderson Ranch Arts Center under the study of renowned artist, William Christanberry. Sarah's artwork has been exhibited extensively in the St. Louis area and she was recently given the Grand Center Visionary Award for Emerging Female Artist of 2006. See more of her work at www.giannobile.net.

Stephen Gibson is author of two poetry collections, *Masaccio's Expulsion*, selected by Andrew Hudgins as winner of The Robert E. Lee and Ruth I. Wilson Poetry Book Award for 2006 from MARGIE/IntuiT House and *Rorschach Art* (Red Hen Press, 2001). His fiction collection, *The Persistence of Memory*, was a finalist for The Flannery O'Connor Award and the Spokane Prize.

Kathleen Hellen's work has appeared in *Earth's Daughters, Iris, Natural Bridge, Nimrod International, The Pacific Review, Prairie Schooner, Southern Poetry Review, Sycamore Review, Rattapallax, RUNES, Seattle Review,* and other journals. Awards include the Thomas Merton Prize for Poetry of the Sacred.

Robert Herschbach's poems have appeared recently in *The Café Review*, *The Louisville Review*, and *Southern Poetry Review* and are forthcoming in *Fugue* and *Fine Madness*. He received his Ph.D. in English from the University of New Hampshire and his MFA in poetry from the University of Iowa. He lives in Maryland with his wife and two children, and works as an editor.

Chris Huntington currently works in the medium-security prison once home to Mike Tyson—but, in his heart, he still wanders the earth like a half-Chinese Davy Crockett. His memoir of life in Africa, Taiwan, and Paris is half-finished and, he says, seems to resemble nothing so much as "a crown of nightingales" or a strange and glorious daydream.

Jennifer Hurley teaches creative writing online at Ohlone College in the San Francisco Bay area. Her stories have appeared in *Mississippi Review*, *Peaks & Valleys*, and *The Green Hills Literary Lantern*.

R. Kimm was born in Washington State in 1941, just prior to Pearl Harbor. After graduating high school in 1959, he joined in the U.S. Army and served in Germany as a translator. He has lived in and around Syracuse, New York since 1977 and is a poet, reviewer, and visual artist.

Mark Neely's poems have appeared in *Indiana Review*, *Salt Hill*, *North American Review*, *Third Coast*, and elsewhere. He teaches at Ball State University in Muncie, Indiana, where he lives with his wife—writer Jill Christman—and their daughter.

Linda Tomol Pennisi has published two collections of poetry, *Seamless* (Perugia Press, 2003) and *Suddenly, Fruit* (Carolina Wren Press, 2006). Her work has appeared or will appear in journals such as *McSweeney's*, *Hunger Mountain*, *Runes*, and *Bellevue Literary Review*. She directs the Creative Writing Program at Le Moyne College in Syracuse, N.Y.

Allan Peterson is the author of two books: *All the Lavish in Common* (2005 Juniper Prize) and *Anonymous Or* (Defined Providence Press) and four chapbooks. Recent print and online appearances include *Prairie Schooner*, *Blackbird*, *Bellingham Review*, *Perihelion*, *Stickman Review*, *Marlboro Review*, and *Massachusetts Review*. A free downloadable chapbook, "*Any Given Moment,*" is available from right handpointing.com

Joseph Radke teaches writing in Milwaukee, WI. His poems have appeared in *Boulevard, Versal, Poetry East, Midwest Quarterly,* and several other journals. *Salt&Sand,* his poetry manuscript, seeks a publisher.

Nina Ronstadt holds an MFA in fiction from the University of Alabama. Her short stories have appeared in *descant* and *America West Airline's Magazine.* She recently completed a novel *Dark Water Ranch,* which has received awards from San Diego State University Writers' Conference and the Taos Summer Writers' Conference. She is married and has two daughters.

Ron Savage has been publishing stories since age eighteen. Recent publications include *Jaberwock Review, Film Comment, G. W. Review, Review,* and *Southern Humanities Review.* Ron has a BA and MA in psychology and a Doctorate in counseling from The College of William and Mary. He has worked as an actor, a broadcaster, a newspaper editor, and for twenty-something years as Psychologist Senior at Eastern State Hospital in Williamsburg. He has recently retired from everything but writing and his wife, Jan.

Catherine Sherman lives in southwestern Pennsylvania and holds degrees from Bennington College, the University of Virginia, and James Madison University. She currently works as the director of academic advising and teaches in the Freshman Forum at Washington & Jefferson College.

Laurel Smith is the co-author of a book of criticism, *Early Works by Modern Women Writers: Woolf, Bowen, Mansfield, Cather, and Stein* (Mellen Press, 2006). Smith's poems have appeared in *New Millennium Writings, JAMA, North Central Review, English Journal,* and in the anthology, *Visiting Frost* (2005). Smith teaches at Vincennes University, in southern Indiana.

Irving Weiss's collection of visual poetry, *Visual Voices: The Poem as a Print Object,* appeared in 1994. He has also been translating Malcom de Chazal for many years, and published two selective translations of *Sens-Plastique* since 1979, the first with preface by W. H. Auden.

River Styx presents the premiere

SCHLAFLY BEER
MICRO-
FICTION
contest

Submit your best micro-fiction and compete to **win a $1000 First Prize** plus two cases of micro-brewed **Schlafly Beer** – winner's choice of ale, stout, or barleywine.

RULES:

500 words maximum per story, up to three stories per entry.

$20 entry fee also buys one year subscription to *River Styx*.

Include name and address on cover letter only.

Entrants notified by S.A.S.E.

Winners published in our April issue.

River Styx editors will select winners.

All stories considered for publication.

MICRO-BREW ☾ MICRO-FICTION

Send stories and S.A.S.E. by December 31st to:
River Styx's Schlafly Beer Micro-fiction Contest
3547 Olive Street, Suite 107
St. Louis, Missouri 63103
www.riverstyx.org • www. schlafly.com

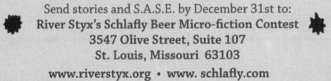

GEORGE CORE, Editor
LEIGH ANNE COUCH, Managing Editor
The University of the South

*H*aving never missed an issue in 115 years, the *Sewanee Review* is the oldest continuously published literary quarterly in the country. Begun in 1892 at The University of the South in Sewanee, Tennessee, the *Review* is devoted to American and British fiction, poetry, and reviews—as well as essays in criticism and reminiscence. In this venerable journal you'll find the direct literary line to Flannery O'Connor, Robert Penn Warren, Hart Crane, Anne Sexton, Harry Crews, and Fred Chappell—not to mention Andre Dubus and Cormac McCarthy, whose first stories were published in the *Sewanee Review*. Each issue is a brilliant seminar, an unforgettable dinner party, an all-night swap of stories and passionate stances.

Published quarterly in Winter, Spring, Summer, and Fall. Volume 115 (2007).

Prepayment is required. **Annual subscriptions:** $25.00, individuals (print or online); $20.00, students (with copy of student I.D.); $34.00, institutions (print or online); $47.60 (print & online). **Foreign postage:** $8.60, Canada & Mexico; $13.00, outside North America. **Single issues:** $8.00, individuals; $10.00, institutions. Payment must be drawn on a U.S. bank in U.S. dollars or made by international money order. **Sales tax:** Residents of CT, DC, GA, and MD add applicable sales tax. For orders shipped to Canada add 6% GST (#124004946RT). Print ISSN: 0037-3052.

Send orders to: The Johns Hopkins University Press
P.O. Box 19966
Baltimore, MD 21211-0966, U.S.A.

For inquiries, email: jrnlcirc@press.jhu.edu. To order using American Express, Discover, MasterCard, or Visa, call toll-free: 1-800-548-1784, outside the U.S. call non-toll-free: 410-516-6987, fax: 410-516-3866, or order online: www.press.jhu.edu/journals

 Published by THE JOHNS HOPKINS UNIVERSITY PRESS

EJHUJ2007

Image: Snow & time ice covering the Smokies (detail); from NOAA Historic NWS Collection, #wea00119; photographer: Grant W. Goodge

If you're going to subscribe to one literary journal this year, subscribe to Natural Bridge.
-LITERARY MAGAZINE REVIEW

poetry ~ fiction ~ essays ~ translations

PUBLISHED TWICE A YEAR: $15/1 YEAR, $25/2 YEARS
UNIVERSITY OF MISSOURI - ST. LOUIS ~ ENGLISH DEPARTMENT
ONE UNIVERSITY BLVD. ~ ST. LOUIS, MO 63121
www.umsl.edu/~natural

Natural Bridge

a Journal of Contemporary Literature

SUBSCRIBE

Natural Bridge Literary Journal publishes
the finest fiction, poetry, personal essays,
and literature in translation by both
emerging and established writers.
Natural Bridge is published two times
a year. Subscriptions:

SUPPORT

I'd like to be reading Natural Bridge.
My check or money order to Natural Bridge is enclosed.

__ One year ($15)   __ Two-years ($25)

__ Donor ($30–$99)   __ Patron ($100–$250)   __ Benefactor ($250 & up)

Name

Address

City, State, Zip

Phone

Return to: Natural Bridge Subscriptions
University of Missouri–St. Louis
Department of English
One University Blvd.
St. Louis, MO 63121-4499